Miss Matched Hearts

MADDIE JAMES

SAND DUNE BOOKS

Miss Matched Hearts

Maddie James

A Sweet Hart Inn Romance, Book 6

About Sweet Hart Inn

Welcome to Sweet Hart Inn... Where the kitchen is always warm and love is always on the menu.

Nestled on the peaceful edge of Falls Lake in the heart of the Blue Ridge Mountains, Sweet Hart Inn is more than a cozy bed and breakfast—it's a place where hearts heal, friendships form, and romance is served with a side of sass.

At the center of it all is Suzie Hart, a chef-turned-innkeeper whose recipes have a way of bringing people together (and finding their way into her books) —and sometimes, sparking unexpected love. Along with her (soon-to-be, maybe?) husband Brad, Suzie welcomes a delightful cast of characters through the inn's front doors, such as runaway brides, brooding bachelors, holiday guests, disgruntled daters, and more.

Whether you're looking for a heartwarming holiday escape, a second-chance romance, or a cozy story filled with culinary charm, the Sweet Hart Inn series delivers all the feel-good vibes you crave.

Bon appétit! And enjoy.

Miss Matched Hearts

Sweet Hart Inn Romance, Book 6

Becca North doesn't want a boyfriend, but Suzie Hart's matchmaking cooking show has other ideas.

Becca North is so over men. Her best friend, Nora, however, treats dating like a sport—and when she ropes Becca into joining a matchmaking segment on Suzie Hart's brand-new cooking show, Becca has no choice but to play along.

Suzie's plan? A romantic blind date picnic featuring Nora.

The problem? Nora's date has eyes for Becca.

Enter Sam Ackerman, landscaper and childhood friend of Suzie's, reluctantly dragged into the scheme. He's sworn off relationships, but one look at Becca has him reconsidering everything. With Suzie's matchmaking magic stirring up more than just recipes, sparks fly where no one expected them—and Becca must decide if love can bloom when she least wants it.

Miss Matched Hearts is a heartwarming, small-town romance sprinkled with cooking show antics, bookshop charm, and an unexpected match. Perfect for readers who love:

- A bookish heroine with no time for love,
- A reluctant hero caught off guard by romance,
- Matchmaking mayhem on a cooking show set,
- Quirky small-town friends, picnics, and plenty of heart.

Local Celebrity Chef To Sign First Cookbook

HARBOR FALLS, NC: Chef Suzie Hart, owner of the popular Harbor Falls Sweet Hart Inn, will sign her debut cookbook, *The Best of Sweet Hart Inn*, Sunday afternoon from 2-4 p.m. at Nora's Novel Niche, a local book venue.

Suzie has owned and operated Sweet Hart Inn for two years. Known for her Hearty & Healthy breakfasts, Suzie signed with an agent to publish the cookbook last year. Aside from running her bed-and-breakfast and working on her next cookbook, she conducts cooking classes at the Inn on Saturdays and caters local and regional events with her cousin Sydney Hart, owner of *Sugar High Coffee Stop* in Harbor Falls.

A former sous chef for the Mountain View Resort Hotel outside of Asheville, a Blue Ridge Mountains landmark, Suzie works alongside her husband, Brad Matthews, keep the cooking business all in the family. Brad Matthews is the owner and Chef de Cuisine of Falls Lake Lodge located on Falls Mountain.

Nora Patterson, owner of Nora's Novel Niche, is preparing for a record crowd. According to a press release issued by Ms. Hart's New York publicist, an announcement regarding an upcoming television opportunity is forthcoming.

Chapter One

"Are you looking for an annual or a perennial?"

That sounded like a question she should know the answer to but didn't. Looking the salesgirl in the eye, Rebecca North replied, "Annual?"

"Sounds like you're not certain."

How she hated being clueless. "You're right. I don't know. An annual sounds like something I should make an appointment for with my doctor."

The young girl laughed. "Well, you are sort of on the right track. You go to your doctor once a year, right? That's annually. So a plant that is an annual only comes up once."

"Once a year?"

"No. Once."

"Sounds like it should be once a year."

"That's a perennial."

"Huh?"

"It comes up and keeps coming up year after year."

"Oh." Confusing. But sounded like what she needed to get her mother for her birthday. Something that kept coming back. The gift that kept on giving. "That's what I want then."

Turning, the girl pointed to the left of the nursery. This was the first time Becca had been to Haven's Hill Nursery at Falls Lake. She knew her mother loved the place—she was always talking about 'running out to Haven's Hill' so Becca felt like she could find something here to please her. Her mother also talked about the two local brothers who owned the place and how she adored them both. Haven's Hill was the horticulture side of the business, where they grew and sold plants and all that entails—you know, like soil, fertilizer, gardening tools, and such. Falls Lake Landscaping was, well, the landscaping wing. She wondered if each of the brothers specialized in one side or the other. Shrugging, she glanced around the place, wondering where those brothers were about now.

Becca knew nothing about plants. She knew books.

"The perennials are all back there," the girl finally said, "next to the trees and shrubbery."

"Which would also be perennial?"

She grimaced. "I suppose you could say that."

Maybe she should get her mother a tree. You can plant trees in the spring, right? Glancing back to the girl, who had now disappeared, she sighed. She'd ask questions later. Right now, perhaps the best thing she could do was act as if she knew what she was doing, and wander about finger plant leaves or something.

She had to get a gift today. Her mother's birthday shindig was tonight.

Thing was, she had no clue where to start. Becca was a bookworm, not a gardener. Her mother had always had such a nicely landscaped lawn, with flowers and beautiful plants everywhere. Becca's tiny, second-story apartment in a Victorian in Old Harbor Falls afforded her space only for a houseplant or two—both gifts from her mother. She was lucky to keep those babies alive.

She wandered the aisles of green, stopped once in a while to fidget with a feathery frond or bend to read the plant names on plastic tabs, only to realize that she still hadn't a clue what she was doing.

About the time she was ready to head out, having decided that perhaps yet again she'd get her mother a book she wouldn't read instead—at least Becca knew books!—she turned to find herself crowded up against a strong, male chest. A chest that wasn't budging.

"Help you find something?" the chest said.

Becca swallowed hard.

Well, actually, it wasn't the chest that spoke, but the mouth attached to the face above the chest. However, somehow, Becca's hands had ended up splayed flat on that chest and she could feel a quiet thump-thump-thump of what must have been his heartbeat against her palms. At once, her own heart echoed that thump-thump-thump, and she worried it was beating so loudly, that the chest, uh, man in front of her, would hear it.

This all happened in like one-point-two seconds.

Her gaze slowly lifted and she met twinkling, hazel eyes.

"Annual," she said. "Uh. I mean perennial."

"Hm. Maybe I can help."

"Plant."

He chuckled. "Excuse me?"

"Need a plant. For my mother. Birthday." What the hell had happened to her speaking ability?

He half-grinned. "I'm sure we can find something."

He backed away, and Becca finally breathed. Her arms dropped lazily to her sides. He took a few steps to his left, and she watched his T-shirted, tight-jeaned body twist and bend— did she really cock her head to the side watching as he did so? —and come up with a nice looking flat of colorful flowers.

"Pretty." She wasn't talking about the blooms.

"Thanks."

"What are they?"

"Pansies. They're hardy."

Hardy. Sounded like another term she didn't know the definition of. "Oh."

"Yes. They'll come back again in the spring."

Are you hardy? Will you come back again in the spring?

Becca shook herself. He was a man. A pretty man, nonetheless, and she had had her fill of pretty men of late. All men, actually. In her world, men didn't come back in the spring, or after the third date, or call the next morning after... Well, it wasn't that bad but she didn't want to think about men right now. This specimen, however, was, ah, intriguing. Even though he looked to be at least a dozen years her senior. Why he would spark her interest, sort of, she didn't know. And why would she expect he might be interested in a barely out of college bookworm?

Where the hell was this line of thought leading her, anyway?

She didn't know. And he'd given her no indication, really, that he was interested. Just tossed her a half-grin and offered up a peek at his tight buttocks. Perhaps he flirts with all his customers. He had flirted, hadn't he?

Perhaps he was just a nice older man.

Somehow she didn't think he would like being referred to as an older man.

He sat the flat down on a wooden counter, lifted one plant from the tray, and held it toward her. "Here. Take a look."

Her hands went out. She took the plant and his big hands covered hers. Warmth raced from her knuckles to her face.

Good Lord am I blushing?

Swallowing hard, she looked again into his eyes, noted a shock of dark brown hair hanging over the right one, and registered the roguish grin on his face. "You know a lot about flowers," she told him.

"I should. I own this place."

Her brow arched. Ah, a brother. Well there you go. No wonder her mother loved this place. "Oh? Congratulations. Nice place. My mother comes here often."

"You're mother has good taste."

"She knows plants."

"Maybe I know her."

Well shit. Probably. "Um, maybe. Trudy North?"

The brother threw back his head and laughed. "Trudy? Well yes! She's a regular. Love her dearly."

Becca didn't understand his laughter. "Why is that funny?"

The humor on his face melted into something half-serious. "No worries. Just struck me as funny that a woman like Trudy has a daughter who is clueless about gardening. Trudy is a master."

Trudy North was good at all kinds of things, especially gardening. "True." She lifted her chin. "I am an anomaly in the family. My dad was a farmer. My mother loves dirt under her fingernails. I, on the other hand...."

Becca glanced down at her acrylic nails. His hands were still cupping hers. He said, "Somehow that interest didn't get passed along to you, did it?"

Becca shook her head. "I know books. English major. I don't know plants."

"I can teach you." His balmy smile lit up his face again, melted something in her chest. "That is, if you are interested."

Interested? In what, plants? Him? What was happening here? She didn't do this sort of thing. Well, not true, lately.... "Oh."

Shifting his stance, he stepped closer. "How about this?

You can teach me about books. I can teach you about plants. Sounds like a date. How about tomorrow night?"

Shit. *Shit!* What a flirt. Date? Tomorrow? What would her mother think? Hell, her mother would love it if she dated one of the Haven's Hill brothers.

Suddenly *The Vow* hit her and she'd be damned if she'd back out on it. If anything, it was a good excuse to ditch his date offer. She'd promised her best friend, Nora, and by God, she was sticking to her vow because she wanted *Nora* to stick to *her* vow. Becca had to set a good example.

They were off men. Too many miscues and too much heartache. Men were the culprit, they had decided, and so with sister bonds and over appetizers and martinis they had made the pact. Stated the vow. Swearing off men from here to eternity.

Nora had pledged. Becca was going to hold her to it.

Nora had been hurt one too many times by pretty men who promised lots and took away even more. Nora needed a break. And Becca? Even if she had to sacrifice the one promising flirty encounter she'd had in weeks in the process, was going to stick to her guns.

There. She could do this.

His fingers clasped her hands a little tighter, and he traced small circles over her knuckles. *Oh, please don't do that...*

She wriggled one hand away and fiddled with the little plastic thingy sticking in the pot. "I'm sure I can read this and figure out what to do with them, and I, um, have plans for Saturday. Sorry."

The guy frowned and then dropped his hands. "Of course."

Perhaps that was too blunt.

He grinned then. "Can't blame a guy for trying. Right?"

Becca ignored that. "I'll just get these," she said, uncertain whether or not her mother would like them.

"I'll carry them to the front checkout for you." Without a second's hesitation, he took the small pot from her hand and added it to the flat. She watched from behind as he carried her purchase to the cash register.

Sigh. Yes. Nice butt.

But she was off men. Even men with nice butts.

She had no clue what to do with hardy pansies and hoped her mother did.

The cute owner spoke briefly to the salesgirl—the one who had pointed her to the perennials moments earlier—and then nodded to her with an obligatory smile and a nod. The flirty guy was gone. Her heart sank.

Well, what did she expect? He had come on rather strong there at the end. What the heck did *he* expect? She wasn't a floosy, after all. Well, usually. That unexpected one-night stand a couple of weeks ago notwithstanding. But her online-match date was nice, and interested in her it seemed, and they'd had a great time at the concert, and then the wham-bam in his car....

Then whoosh. Nothing.

Dropped her off and drove away.

No call. No text. No nothing.

She rolled her eyes. Men. Of course, this was partly her fault.

But no matter. All's well that ends well. This temptation was over and she had maintained the integrity of *The Vow*. Disaster averted.

THE NEXT DAY, Sam Ackerman angled his shovel at the ground, gave it a hefty thrust, and then kicked the back of it pushing the blade deep into the soil. It wasn't that he was frustrated, but there was no doubt he was tired. Suzie Hart rattled on behind him.

"No, no," she said. "I was thinking of moving the hostas over there. The sun eats them up like crazy on this side of the house. I think they need more shade."

That's what I told you when we planted them there.

Thank goodness, they had worked in some sand and topsoil to the hard-packed clay soil around Suzie's house last year—an excellent decision on his and his brother's part—or the job would have been a lot more difficult. And thank God the hostas were young, just a few months in the ground and not yet established. Easier to move to the other side of the house.

Where I wanted to put them last year.

"Sam, thank you for being tolerant with me."

Grinning at the ground, he raised his face to meet Suzie's infectious smile. "No problem, darlin'."

She caught his gaze. "I know sometimes I'm a pain in the ass," she said. "And you know that if I could get all of this done myself, I would do it. It's just that I've been so crazy busy the past months and I've let the landscaping and gardening slip. Once we get it spruced up, and I get this book tour out of the way, I'll be ready to settle back in and keep things up. You know how I love the place to look in the spring."

"And in the summer, fall, winter..." He did indeed. Sweet Hart Inn was Suzie's baby and he was happy to be her landscaper. His heart warmed and any annoying thoughts about moving the hostas dissipated. Childhood friends since elementary school, he could never be mad at her for long. "Hey, that's what you pay Jack and me for. To do the things you can't get to, honey."

A corner of her mouth turned up. "You guys know what I want and how I want it to look."

Obviously. And we were right about the hostas.

"Besides, you're the best." She reached out and laid a hand on his forearm. "I wouldn't have anyone but Haven's Hill landscape my property. Oh, hey, and I mentioned you all in my blog the other day. I hope it brings you some more local business."

Well, that was mighty sweet of her. Now, it was time to get back to moving the plants, pruning back a few trees and bushes, and readying the beds for winter. "Well, hon, that's exactly what we aim to do, please our friends and customers."

Again, Suzie smiled. "You're a godsend." Glancing about, she added. "Wow, I really did add to your workload here today, didn't I? And it's getting late. Were you planning to finish today, or can you come back tomorrow?"

"What time is it?"

"Nearly five."

"Oh." He'd lost track of the time. Sam kicked the shovel into the ground again and pulled back on the handle to loosen the soil around the root ball. Glancing up, he surveyed the clear blue sky behind her head. "I think we're safe to put the rest of this off until tomorrow if okay with you. Weather is supposed to be good another day."

"Fine with me." She reached for a basket sitting at her feet. "Got a date tonight? It is Saturday."

"Hell no." Date. No.

Suzie laid a hand on his arm. "Sam Ackerman, it's Saturday night! Go out and find a girl and have some fun!"

"No, thanks. I'm looking forward to a cold beer on your deck and looking out over the lake, followed by a slow drive home, a nice hot shower when I get there, and an early bedtime."

"Sam, that makes me so sad."

Funny, it didn't make him sad at all. Women weren't in the cards right now and it was okay. Hell, even the innocent flirting he'd done yesterday with the one woman who had stepped into his nursery that had stirred a bit of interest, or something, in him, had gotten him shot down. Thing was, he was probably coming on a little stronger than he normally would have, but the sassy little minx had caught his eye and just wouldn't let go.

Truth be known, he was still thinking about her.

Smiling, he grasped her hand. "Hey, don't worry about me. I'm perfectly happy with my mundane, solitary life. I'm too damned busy right now to add a woman to it. Maybe down the road some."

"I just hate it that you and Carol Jean broke up."

"It's okay, Suzie. These things happen."

She sighed. "Well. Just as long as you haven't given up on women altogether."

"No ma'am." Well, he hoped, anyway. He and Carol Jean had ended a few months ago and he had to admit, he'd felt like giving up on love when it had. He'd loved her—he thought anyway—until he'd overheard her talking to a girlfriend at local BBQ cookout, and realized the woman had been lying to him for a while and she didn't know how to tell him the truth about something. Yeah, one lie and then another and before he knew it, she was not the woman he thought she was. He broke it off. She cried. He vowed he wasn't going there again anytime soon.

In reality and with hindsight, they both realized it was for the best. It never would have worked. He just wished she had come clean sooner and hadn't wasted both of their time.

"Just waiting for the right woman, Suzie."

"Good. Well, just don't wait too long. And if she doesn't come along, then let me know. I'll fix you up, Sam. They *are* calling me *The Matchmaking Chef* these days, you know?"

He snorted. He had heard that. Might as well go with it and change the subject. "Okay, Suze. Hey look, we'll be back tomorrow, sometime after church, all right?"

"Sure." She fiddled with some tools in the basket. "I have a book signing at two in town at the bookstore so will be gone for a while—oh, from about noon until six or so, I think. Brad and Petey will be with me, but you know where we keep everything. The shed will be unlocked if you need anything."

"Sounds good."

"I hate to make you work on a Sunday."

He grinned. "Suzie, you know I'd be working somewhere anyway. I love what I do. And besides, it's supposed to rain Monday."

She nodded. "I do know you love your job. Didn't know about the rain. Bummer."

"No problem, Suzie." He watched her stroll down the length of her house inspecting the plants. Truth was, plants and landscaping were his passion. He'd not wanted to do anything else since he was a kid growing up on his parents' farm. Biggest reason he'd gone to college was to major in Agriculture, then quite by surprise, he found his way into a horticulture class which opened up another entire world for him. What surprised him most was that his younger brother, Jack, had followed in his footsteps. Haven's Hill Nursery at Falls Lake was ten years old and prospering, largely because he and Jack did a lot of the grunt work, alongside his crews. Hey, it kept him fit and tan, and he'd heard the girls liked that.

Girls. He was thirty-five. Women, not girls. But just where were all the available women in Harbor Falls? The ones who didn't come with baggage or lied?

Nowhere.

Hell, he was probably going to have baggage himself over that last woman.

The blonde from yesterday, though, was definitely young and he didn't know her. Was she from Harbor Falls? From somewhere else? He was old and she was too young for him. Maybe she was still in college yet even. Hell, that's why he didn't know her she was practically from another generation.

Where the hell was his head? She probably thought him a dirty old man. Shit.

"So we're moving the hostas?"

Sam swiped his brow. Jack had joined him, and Suzie was now ambling off toward her wildflower garden with a pair of scissors in one hand and her basket in the other. "Could have predicted that."

Jack chuckled. "Here. Let's get this done. Maybe we can con her into a cold one on her deck before we leave."

"I was counting on that."

Both men started digging.

BECCA GRIMACED and twitched her nose. A smoky smell wafted up from the canister of, um, were those supposed to be chocolate chip cookies? Without a sound, she replaced the metal lid, turned away, and sighed.

"I so wanted a chocolate chip cookie," she muttered, then reached to straighten the counter area around her. Bookmarks. Sales fliers. A tabletop cardboard display of Jed McDermott's latest paperback release. "But not one of those burnt things. Definitely, not one of those."

She shook herself a little and eased out behind the counter, straightening a nearby end cap. "Face out," she said as she turned several copies of her favorite suspense author, Brit Calloway's latest, *Born to Run*, out to show the cover. "Face in," she echoed, feeling only semi-bad about turning an unknown author's books around, making them disappear into the fold. "Slow. Ass. Day."

She enjoyed working at the bookstore. Truly she did. But she looked forward to the day she could put her degree to good use in a slightly different manner. Perhaps writing ad copy for an advertising firm. Or maybe even working her way into a position as a journalist in a small newspaper. Something a little faster-paced and edgy. Often her days at the bookstore were too long and slow—but no matter, tomorrow was going to be a doozy.

Behind her, the hard click of heels tatting across the tile floor met her ear. She'd know that walk anywhere. "Hi, Nora."

"Hey." A tired-sounding whoosh and a scrape of metal against metal came next. Becca rotated back toward the counter and found her childhood best friend, former college roommate, and owner of Nora's Novel Niche, leaning a hip against the counter and nibbling a burnt cookie. "Good party for your mom last night, Bec."

"It was okay." She'd never again buy plants for her mother. How could she have known that her mother already planted dozens of pansies the day before? And icing on the cake, she'd been bothered all evening because she'd been too abrupt with Mr. Gardener Man back at the nursery. Even though it was for the best. She sure hoped her mother didn't get wind of it, being that Haven's Hill was her favorite nursery and all. So far today she had kept her distraction to a minimum, but for some odd reason those hazel eyes of his kept sneaking back into her consciousness. "Ready for tomorrow?" Changing the subject was always an option.

A wrinkle waved over Nora's forehead.

"Something wrong?"

"Worried as hell about the book signing."

"As long as you don't serve those cookies, things will go fine."

"What?"

"Seriously, you've seen to every detail. I can't imagine what could go wrong."

Nora pulled the cookie away from her mouth and looked at it. "Wow. I thought these were pretty darned good. Baked them late last night. I love a crisp cookie."

Frowning, Becca shivered again. Those gems were beyond crisp. "I prefer chewy."

"To each their own."

"Just like men, huh?"

Nora sputtered and crumbs flew. "That's not a subject I want to get into today." Still chewing, she tossed the remainder of her cookie into a wastebasket under the counter and snapped the lid back on the can. "Men," she continued, "are the furthest thing from my mind. Men, are like, off my 'to do' list. Men, are pretty much nonexistent in my book. In fact," she glanced around, "the word man is not even in my vocabulary anymore."

Becca didn't want to get into the subject either, especially since her encounter from yesterday lingered on her mind. She'd not had a *serious* boyfriend in ages—not since her college days—and truth be told, she really didn't care if she had one for some time. Oh, she dated occasionally and had tried out the matching sites, but generally those didn't end well. Besides, men just seemed to complicate her life. They screwed with her head and made her think and do things she normally wouldn't do.

Like with Concert Dude. What had gotten into her?

He was cute. Sexy. Smiled at her a lot. And she'd been enamored. So she'd caved and well, now she regretted it.

That thought affirmed her bluntness with Mr. Gardener Man—although she didn't think he was anything like Concert Dude.

Nora didn't feel the same about men, though. Nora really, *really* wanted a man in her life. Her career was set, her father having left the bookstore to her when he had retired. Now, she was all about the happily-ever-after. You know, searching for it, finding the man of her dreams, settling down with kids and dogs and a picket fence. Heck, the romance section was the largest genre section in the bookstore! Thing was, romance always seemed to elude Nora, no matter how hard she tried.

And she tried hard. Believe you, me.

But she needed a pause after her last breakup, and so, yes, they'd vowed the other evening over martinis and fried calamari that they were off men. For a while. Becca silently bet that she could outlast Nora with that vow.

Because Nora was always looking. It was instinctual.

Becca, on the other hand, had convinced herself lately that she'd rather stay home and watch a movie or read a book alone, than invite some man into her life who would upset her perfect little apple cart life. Because that, indeed, had happened to her while in college—and she wondered why she occasionally risked getting into that kind of scenario again. Her sweetheart had literally taken over her life for most of their college years—until they graduated, and he found a nice busty blonde in graduate school that met his needs a little more fully.

And that was exactly what he had told Becca. She didn't meet his needs anymore.

Asshole.

Talk about a blow to the ego. But no matter. She was better off. Without a man in her life, she was in control. But this was about Nora, not Becca. Nora, bless her heart, was constantly on the search.

"Men are not in my vocabulary either," she told her friend.

Nora smirked and began shuffling things around on the counter—the very things that Becca had just straightened moments earlier. Nervous. She could tell with that tic of Nora's lip and the twitch of her hands as they fidgeted over the items like nobody's business. After all, they'd been best friends since high school and lived together in the dorm for four years after that.

To say they knew each other well was an understatement.

Nora's jumpiness was probably what kept her so damned thin. Becca gave her friend the once-over. In fact, Nora appeared thinner than normal. She always lost weight when something was preying on her mind. Becca actually envied her of that fact. She, herself, always grew a little pudgy around the middle when she was stressed. But Nora was always beautiful. Beautiful blond hair, blue-eyed, thin, and long legs to die for.

Becca was the exact opposite in most every respect.

While she was also blond, hers was dirtier and darker. Her green eyes were unique, but her pale complexion with freckles clearly gave away her Irish heritage. Which wasn't a bad thing either. She was short—her five-foot-two frame was supported by the thighs of a gymnast. Came from all of that bicycling she did as a kid, she guessed. And hardy—if she could use a term often used for plants—she was probably that. German stock on her Grandmother's side. Irish on her grandfather's. Oh, she supposed she was okay to look at on a good day, but Nora was always the one who caught the attention of the boys when they were in school.

Or later, men, at a bar.

Or in the mall.

Or at any-sort-of-social-event-that-the-two-of-them-would-go-to-together.

Nora was always the main course. Becca was the side dish. *Sigh.*

Therefore, it wasn't that Nora was homely or anything, that put men off. Quite the opposite. If Becca had to define it, she'd be pressed to say that perhaps Nora was a mite too eager. It sent a lot of men running for the hills, um, mountains. Nora often didn't realize how she came off until the next best relationship fell through and she was crying in her martini, not understanding where it went wrong.

It was an ugly cycle Becca had hoped to get her best friend out of, but to no avail. Honestly, picking up after Nora's disaster-of-a-love life left her very little time to concentrate on one of her own, which she didn't want, anyway.

What a convoluted mess!

About then, the front door opened with a chime, and they turned toward the sound. Becca watched Nora's profile as she took in the tall, dark-headed, and oh-so-handsome stranger who sauntered in. Immediately her chin lifted, her back straightened, and a hand fluttered to her chest. She swallowed and cocked her head to one side. Looking.

Becca stepped up beside her and whispered. "He doesn't exist. Not in your vocabulary."

"Dammit."

"You need a man like you need a hole in the head."

"Keep reminding me." Her stare never left the man, who had shifted toward the Business section. From their vantage point, they had a good look at his backside.

Becca bent her head in the same direction as Nora's. Together, both women sighed. "Nice..."

"Agreed."

The man twisted and looked at the women. They immediately shifted and fiddled with things on the counter.

"We're off men," Becca said a little louder, removing the cookie tin from the counter and stashing it underneath.

"Ditto." Nora started rearranging the countertop display again. "Let's think about something else."

"What about the book signing tomorrow? Anything I can help with?"

Nora exhaled as if she had been holding that breath for days.

Becca noticed the worry lines etching deeper across her friend's forehead again. There, that got her mind off the man.

"I think all is ready," she said. "I didn't realize this was going to be such a big deal! I had no clue that this woman from Harbor Falls had developed this big following. The television people are going to be here from Asheville *and* the author's New York publicist *and* we had to order more books yesterday. I hope they get here in time. Had them overnighted, which cost me a bundle so I sure as hell hope they sell. People will start lining up early, I assume." She drummed her fingers on the counter and looked Becca straight in the eyes. "Just keep me sane, Becca. This could be the best thing to hit my bookstore ever. With the current economy, we need the business and the promotional opportunity. Oh, God! I'm so excited!"

"Ahem."

Becca pulled her gaze away from Nora's animated face to look at the man from the Business section, who was now standing at the register holding a book on project management. "Good afternoon, sir," she said. "Thank you for shopping at Nora's!"

Taking the book from him, Becca scanned his purchase while he thoroughly scanned Nora. See? Their eyes always went straight to Nora—who was now preening like a peacock. "I can't believe you didn't know about Suzie Hart," she said to Nora while nudging her side, and changing the subject. "She's been a local sensation for a while. Haven't you ever had breakfast at her Inn?"

Nora didn't answer. Becca finished ringing up the sale and put the book in a paper bag. She glanced at Nora who was smiling at the man and twiddling a lock of hair with her thumb and forefinger.

Becca nudged her again.

Nora turned. "What?"

She whispered the reminder. "Not in your vocabulary."

"My wife loves Suzie Hart," the man interjected. "She's been taking her cooking classes lately and we've not missed one of her Summer Sunrise Breakfasts the past three years."

He smiled at the two. "She will be here with bells on tomorrow, I'm sure."

Becca smiled and handed him his purchase. "That's great news. We look forward to seeing her! Be sure to tell her to say hello."

"Right," Nora replied. Untangling her hair from her fingers, she dropped her hand, and then gave Becca a half-hearted smile and a shrug. "Right."

Becca sighed. Maintaining the vow was going to be hard work.

Chapter Two

"Sam? What happened between you and Carol Jean? If you don't mind me asking."

Sam pulled a shovel and rake out of Suzie's shed and stared into the dark hole of the structure for a few seconds before turning and looking at her. He really did mind but he was too much of a gentleman to ignore her.

"It just didn't work, Suzie."

"I really hate that. She's a sweet girl."

"She is that."

"And you are such a great guy."

"Well, I hope so."

"You made such a cute couple."

"So people said."

"What happened?"

Sam faced her. "Turns out she likes girls better than boys."

He watched Suzie's eyes grow wide. "No."

Nodding, he added. "Oh, yes. Came as a surprise to me too but she's happy as a clam now—or so she tells me. She emails occasionally from Phoenix, where she lives now. With her wife."

"Well, I'll be. I had no clue."

"You're not the only one."

Suzie laid a hand on his forearm. "Now, don't you worry, Sam. I'll help find you a wife of your own. I'm pretty good at it!"

Clearing his throat, Sam squared himself in front of her. "Don't you have a book signing to get to today?"

She smiled and nodded. "I do. And I need to get going. Now, don't you fret, you hear? I'll be thinking about you." She turned and headed back toward her house.

Sam's gut sank. "Suzie!" he called out.

She turned.

"No matchmaking for me. You hear? I'm not into that kind of crap."

Suzie flashed him one of her signature smiles, turned, and sashayed off.

"Crap is right," he muttered to himself. "I need to nip this in the bud ASAP."

PEOPLE WERE LINED up out the door. At the last minute, Nora and Becca decided to conduct a lottery for tickets to attend the press conference prior the book signing. Nora was a freakin' mess. Becca was beside herself trying to keep her best friend from flittering away into nothingness, keeping the fans at bay, and dealing with the publicist and the producer from the new cable cooking station, Channeling Food. The author, Suzie Hart, was surprisingly calm.

"This is mega-big," Becca muttered while watching the surreal scene before her. Nora was chatting with the author in front of the signing table. The television people were setting up lights and microphone booms. A makeup girl was puffing and brushing and flitting around both Suzie and Nora. And the Channeling Food woman was making a beeline straight toward Becca.

Plum. Her name was Patricia Plum. Not usually one to remember names, Becca had decided early on that this one was a keeper in her brain.

"May I help you, Ms. Plum?"

"Water. We need three bottles of water."

She nodded. "Coming right up. I have them chilling in the back." She headed for the storage room. The click of Patricia's heels followed, and she glanced over her shoulder.

"I need a quiet moment, if you don't mind."

"Of course."

Patricia followed her into the storage room.

A minute later, Becca closed the door behind them, shutting out the noise. Moving to the small cooler with bottled water, she reached for one, wiped it off with a paper towel, and handed it to Patricia. She then gathered two more.

Patricia leaned against a shelf and put the icy bottle next to her forehead. "I have one mother of a headache."

Becca understood. She had a wee one herself. "I have something for that. Hold on." With the keys dangling from the lanyard around her neck, she unlocked a filing cabinet drawer and pulled out her purse. From there, she fished around for a bottle of aspirin and handed it to Patricia.

"Thank God. And thank you."

"Bad one?"

Patricia twisted the bottle cap and shook out a couple of white pills. "Bad enough. Stress. Didn't sleep much last night. In fact, haven't slept a lot in weeks." She met Becca's gaze head on, then tossed the pills in her mouth and took a drink of the water. "My entire career is resting on this new show," she added after swallowing.

"Suzie's show?"

"Yes. It's different. It could be a winner or a bust. She's an unknown in New York but I want to give her a shot. Instinct, you know. Feel it in my gut."

"Seems like she's pretty popular around here."

Patricia nodded. "Yes. We have the local angled covered and tied up with a bow, with additional thanks to your boss, Nora. I have to sell her to the nation though. I swindled this new network for a few episodes. I have to make it work. She's got a unique enough angle, I just hope it flies."

Becca wondered what Nora had to do with all of this. The book signing, probably. She didn't realize Suzie had an angle though. She should really pay more attention to the foodie trend, she guessed. "Angle?"

Handing the aspirin bottle back to Becca, she said, "Oh, yes. Suzie is The Matchmaking Chef. Didn't you know? That's her new show. And we're featuring her newly contracted cookbook, *Perfectly Matched* in the deal. Helluva marketing plan. We're even going to feature some of her matchmaking successes on the show and in the book." She glanced at her watch. "Damn. It's almost time. I have to get back out there."

She capped her water bottle and exited the storeroom.

Becca stared after her. Suzie Hart from Harbor Falls was a matchmaker? Who knew?

Quickly, she left the storage room herself and joined the others near the signing table. Nora stepped up beside her, her face beaming. She knew this moment was important for Nora and the store. Becca heard things like, "quiet on the set" and "places, please," and "rolling" and then Suzie was being interviewed for the local television, followed by the television crew taking footage of Suzie's publicist announcing the launch of her book tour. Then, Patricia Plum stepped up to the mic and announced Suzie's new show, *The Matchmaking Chef*, on the new and upcoming cable food channel, Channeling Food.

Nora was practically squirming beside her. Becca glanced

again to her friend's face. Something was going on.

"And we are so happy to share," Patricia went on, "that one of Suzie's first episodes on *The Matchmaking Chef*, will feature recipes from her upcoming cookbook, *Perfectly Matched*, along with a matchmaking episode featuring Harbor Falls very own Nora Patterson, owner of Nora's Novel Niche!"

The crowd clapped and hooted and Nora was waved closer to the camera and mic. She skittered forward, glowing and grinning, and glanced sideways at Becca—who was sure her mouth was hanging six inches from the floor.

The tramp!

LATER, after the book signing was over, the crowd diminished, the camera crew gone, the New York people tucked into a cab headed toward the airport, and Suzie and her cute hubby on their way back to Sweet Hart Inn, Becca looked at her best friend and said, "What in the world are you doing?"

Nora shrugged. "I hired her. Sort of. Well, that's how it started, anyway."

"What?"

"Well, we were talking, Suzie and me, about the matchmaking thing. I was going to hire her to fix me up. We talked about a nice picnic lunch in the mountains. Maybe a blind date. Then that Plum woman overheard us, and the thing started snowballing. Before I knew it, I was signing something that said I agreed to be on an episode. Ack!"

"But you're off men."

"It's just TV. Acting."

"Oh, yeah. Right, Nora."

"Truly!"

"Sounds a bit like reality TV to me."

"Well, maybe a little." One corner of Nora's mouth drew up. "Patricia said I had good looks for television."

Well, of course you do. That's a given.

"And it would be wonderful promotion for the bookstore."

"You've got to be kidding. Are you really doing this?"

"Yes!"

Becca shook her head. "You forgot all about our calamari vow."

"I'm not sure that vows made over calamari and martinis can be taken seriously."

"I took it seriously." *Dammit, I sacrificed a date with Mr. Hunky Gardener.*

Nora stared at her. "Becca, I want a boyfriend! Okay, so I'm breaking the calamari vow."

"Dammit." That time she said it aloud. It came from her own mouth and she wasn't quite sure why. What did it matter if Nora wanted to date? To be on a television show? What was it to her?

Nothing. Absolutely nothing. It didn't change things one bit in Becca's life.

I just don't want to have to pick up the Nora pieces again.

"This is a good thing, Becca. Be happy for me! It will be fun." She jumped a little and twittered about. "Hey! You can come with me. Check him out for me from the side. Give me your advice."

My advice is to steer clear of blind dates!

Becca studied her friend's face. "No, Nora. This is your doing. Don't drag me in the middle of this, you hear? Because I am off men. Totally. I am keeping our calamari vow. You hear me? I am so off dates, especially blind dates, and picnics, and reality TV shows...and men."

Nora gave her a hug and squeeze, her eyes twinkling.

"Sure you are. Got it."

Chapter Three

Easing himself down into a padded lounge chair on Suzie's back deck, Sam exhaled long and stretched his aching legs out over the footrest. His brother, Jack, handed an icy beer his way. "Oh, yeah…" Sam said. "I am so ready for that."

"Just glad this job is done."

"Ditto."

"Figured Brad owed us a beer."

"He'll gladly give up a few beers in exchange for him not moving those hostas around."

"Speak of the Devil."

Both men turned toward the sound of tires crunching on gravel coming up the drive at the side of the house. They watched as Brad and Suzie parked the car and sauntered toward the deck.

"Hey guys," Suzie called out. "Looks like you've been working hard."

"Just a tad," Sam said. "Hey, where's Petey?"

"We dropped him off at my parents. Been a long day for him and us, and I for one am looking forward to a long hot bubble bath," she winked at her husband, "for two."

Sam and Jack glanced away. Sam cleared his throat.

Then Suzie changed the subject. "Oh, everything looks lovely, guys!"

Sam tipped his head. "As I always say, we aim to please, Ms. Famous Cookbook Author."

"And soon to be television personality," Brad added.

Sam sat up. "Television? No joke?"

Suzie nodded. "I'm going to have my own show on a new food channel." Then she did a real girly thing and squealed. "Oh, my God!" She grasped Brad's arm. "I can't believe this!"

Standing now, Sam reached out to shake Brad's hand.

"Well, congratulations there, Mr. Matthews. You've got yourself a TV wife."

Brad smirked and shook his hand. "Just wait. I may not be the only one."

Sam didn't understand that.

Suzie elbowed her husband and gave him a look. Then she turned toward Sam. "I thought about this all the way home, Sam. You're perfect. Perfect! With those biceps and that tan of yours, the camera will eat you up. And so will your date. You have to say yes. It won't take up too much of your time, and it's going to be taped right here in the mountains, so please, just say yes."

Suddenly, Sam was damn certain he didn't like the sinking feeling in his gut. "I don't have a clue what you're talking about."

"I've found you a date. A match! She's perfect for you. And all you need to do is go on a little picnic up in the mountains. A blind date, sure, but you can handle that. Just you and the girl, and me and lunch, and well, the camera crew."

"Camera crew?" Sam backed off, easing his way toward the deck steps. "Oh, no." He didn't need no stinkin' match-maker to get him a girl. "Hey Jack, buddy, it's time to go."

His brother chuckled and stood. "Sounds like this is just getting good."

"Oh, please say yes, Sam! You'll get paid, and you'll be on national television!"

"Hell's bells, Suzie! I'm a gardener from Harbor Falls. I'm not TV material! And I don't want to date on national television!"

"Maybe not," she countered, "but you are husband material. And I'm not taking no for an answer, Sam Ackerman."

Even as he was shaking his head and backing away from Suzie, affirming to himself with each step of the way that he was *not* blind date, television, *or* husband material, he feared that sooner or later, Suzie would bat her Southern Belle eyelashes and get her way.

Dammit.

"I REALLY, really need for you to come with me. Please?"

Shit. Damn. And no freakin' way.

It was Saturday morning, one week after the book signing and Becca was standing in the door of her apartment looking out at Nora. Her friend wore jeans, hot pink rhinestone-studded flip-flops, and a matching pale pink tank top layered over another white tank. Her newly sprayed-on tan perfectly complemented the pastel pink. Her long hair was down, framing her face, her makeup perfection. She looked very, very beautiful.

Like a Barbie doll.

Her date would find her extremely difficult to resist, she was certain.

"You don't need me there, Nora. You're going to do just fine on your own. Besides, Suzie is so easy to deal with, any nervousness you might have she will immediately put at ease.

"I need you, Bec. Please?"

She gave her the famous *don't-make-me-beg* look.

"Crap, Nora! You don't need me hanging around like a third wheel, like some... Er, side dish!"

"Puh-lease?" Nora pouted. "I need you to check him out. You know I have a difficult time with first impressions. I love any man who shows me the least bit of attention. I need an impartial party. I need intel. I need solicited opinions. You know I'm not good at this!"

No, you are not.

Becca felt herself caving. *Sucker.* She raked her fingers through a strand of hair. "I need a shower."

"I'll wait."

"I can meet you."

"I'll wait. Go."

Becca resisted the urge to grumble. "I need thirty minutes."

"We've got plenty of time. Why do you think I got over here so early?"

"Conspiracy."

"You'll love it."

"Doubt that."

"Go, Becca!"

"Sheez!" *Okay, so I'm going. Against my better judgment, but all right. I'll be the side dish. I'll observe from the periphery. I'll tell you later what I think. I won't get involved.*

Won't. Get. Involved.

Repeat.

I won't get involved.

∾

BENEATH A LAZY MAPLE sat a wooden picnic table draped in a bright red and white checked tablecloth. Becca watched, from the sidelines of course, as Suzie set the table with red dishes, white cloth napkins, and wicker accents. From a picnic basket sitting on a table off to the side, she prepared her dishes for the lunch.

Television people milled about, Nora was off being prepped by Ms. Plum, and Becca was perfectly happy to ease out of the chaos while leaning against a tree trunk, far from the maddening crowd.

She watched Nora, who was smiling and giddy. She'd been in contact with both Suzie and Patricia all week, getting pointers on this and that. She'd even had a private lesson with an acting coach just to settle her nerves. The one thing she had not concentrated on too much was the fact that she was going to meet a man—a man who might potentially be her mate. Becca hadn't dwelled on it, either.

Now, however, it weighed on her mind.

On one hand, Becca wanted Nora to find someone who would be perfect for her. And, if Becca would admit it, she truly wanted to be there for Nora, to help her make this decision. On the other hand, she wanted no part of helping Nora to select a mate, because, well, what if she chose wrong? What if her gut instincts about the man were not on track?

She certainly wanted nothing to come between them and their friendship. Mostly she didn't want Nora to get hurt again. So truly, she had no choice here. She would peruse the date. Listen from the sidelines. Take in the nuances of the man. And later, tell Nora exactly what she thought.

"This whole thing is rather crazy, isn't it?"

Jerked out of her musing, Becca glanced to her right and pushed away from the tree.

Holy shit!

Where he came from, she didn't know, but before her stood a man. Tan, tall, and tantalizingly delicious. He was buff

—the kind of buff that made you think he probably got that way from working outside, rather than working out in a gym.

Because, of course, that's what he did. Work outside. Like, in a nursery.

Mr. Gardener Man?

No way! Did he remember her?

Becca sucked in a breath. He stood hands on hips peering back at her. Her gaze lingered for a moment at his waist—crisp white shirt tucked into worn jeans anchored by a brown leather belt at narrow hips—then slipped lower.

Crotch. Muscled thighs. Oh be still my irrational, thumping, pumping heart.

"Yeah, crazy, huh?" Did those words come from her mouth?

Pulling her gaze back up to look into his eyes, her mouth went dry. Hazel, with sunlight reflecting a bit of gold and lavender. Framed by thick lashes and perfectly arched brows, his orbs connected with hers and held. A breeze wafted between them and he reached up to smooth back his tousled, brown hair. His fingers were long, his hands large.

Just as she'd remembered.

Her heart kicked up a steadier beat.

"Where. Wha... Um. Where did you come from?" Did her tongue work?

He shifted and looked over his shoulder. "I came early and parked over there at that camp site. I figured I'd be more comfortable if I could check out the scenario ahead of time before all the hoopla started."

Smart man. Was this...?

"Name's Sam Ackerman." He thrust out his hand. "And you are...?"

Spellbound.

His voice was smooth like really, really good bourbon. She hadn't remembered that. Her hand drifted up and he took it.

"Becca. I'm Becca North," she told him. "I bought pansies."

He snickered and smiled. "I remember. Trudy's daughter."

She bought pansies? Sheesh! "Yes."

His big hand encased hers. Warm. Slightly calloused. Nice. And he was still holding it. Like the other day. "Nice to meet you, Becca." Finally, he broke their grasp. "Officially." Tossing his gaze toward the picnic scene he added, "Are you part of all his?"

He did remember her. "No. I mean. Yes. Well, sort of."

He laughed aloud. Nice, nice laugh. Almost made her smile. Hell, it did make her smile.

"My friend Nora," she pointed toward her, "is part of the show. She's the blonde over there by the table and the one being matchmaked."

Matchmaked? Was that a word?

Sam followed her gaze. "Hm." He watched for a while as Nora listened to Patricia. While he did that, it gave Becca the perfect opportunity to study his profile. Chiseled features, high cheekbones, a slightly scruff dark beard. She bet he got a five o'clock shadow each day.

At some point in her musing, Sam had turned to look into her face again. Their gazes hooked together and held. "It's nice to see you, again."

She glanced at the ground. "I... Yes. Good to see you, too."

Again, their gazes connected. He continued. "I spotted you as soon as I got out of my truck a little while ago. I couldn't believe it was you. I'm glad to have another chance to speak to you."

Becca bit her lip, and then said in a rush. "I'm sorry I was so abrupt the other day. I'm just not used to men asking me out like that."

"Hey. It's not a regular thing for me, either, sweetheart. Kind of took me by surprise."

In the worst way, Becca wanted to smile. Okay, so she did a little. "Really?"

"Yes."

A pause lingered.

"When I saw you a few minutes ago, I couldn't believe my luck. I was sort of hoping it was going to be you."

"What?"

Sam tipped his head toward the crowd around the picnic table. "I'm the date. The other one being matchmaked."

"Ah." *Shit.*

"Yep." He rubbed that scruffy beard. Had he said he wished it had been her?

"I'm sure you will like Nora."

"I think you are more my type."

Panic zinged through her. "Oh, but Nora is smart and beautiful and..."

He interrupted with, "Don't sell yourself short, Becca North. You too are beautiful, and I bet quite smart."

What?

A silly, saucy grin crossed his lips, and her mouth itched to echo it.

"Mr. Ackerman? Is that you?"

Sam glanced away to see who was approaching. Becca looked too. Patricia. Saved by the bell, or rather, the Plum.

"Becca!" she started, "thank goodness you found Mr. Ackerman." Patricia hooked her arm in Sam's and tugged to lead him away. "I have a few things to go over before the lunch and taping, and oh! You must meet Nora before we begin. Minor detail." She giggled and Sam looked over his shoulder back to Becca. "Of course you want to meet her ahead of time. It's a date, right? I mean, we'll pretend it's a blind date and all but what kind of a show would it be if..."

Patricia's voice faded as they strode away. The only good

thing about watching them walk away was that Becca got another perfect view of Sam Ackerman's firm and taut backside.

She did enjoy watching that man walk away.

Chapter Four

"Keep your eyes on your date. On your date! Sam!"

Dammit. Why couldn't he keep his eyes—and his attention—on Nora? She was beautiful with all that long pretty hair and equally long, thin denim-clad legs, and eyes blue as bursting blueberries.

"Cut!"

The crew exhaled, and so did he. "Sorry. This isn't working." Sam tossed his napkin on the table and got up. Swiping the back of his hand across his upper lip, he brushed away a line of sweat. Nerves. And it was hot this afternoon.

They'd gone a lot longer than expected. Couldn't get the right shots.

Nora stepped up beside him. "Sam, are you okay?"

He didn't meet her questioning gaze. "Fine."

"It's me, right?"

Damn. He didn't want her to think that, so he did look at her then. "Oh, no, Nora. It's not you." Those damn blue eyes held all kinds of expectation. Some guy, somewhere, would be thrilled to be in his shoes right now. "It's me. I'm a gardener, not an actor. You're wonderful."

She smiled at the wonderful part.

But you're not as wonderful as your friend over there. He glanced over Nora's shoulder at Becca. Thing was, he was supposed to be focusing his attention on the woman in front of him, not her sweet, sexy, friend hanging out on the fringes.

"We'll just take another break. Here, let me get some water," she offered.

He watched her walk away. Jack would call him every kind of crazy, but he just wasn't into this right now. Water wasn't going to make any difference. This acting gig, or the match-making thing, wasn't for him.

"So what's up, Sam?"

Suzie joined him. His shoulders slumped, and again, he exhaled. Long. Staring her straight in the eyes he said, "I'm cutting out on you, Suzie. It was a great idea, but I'm not your man."

"You can't do that to me, Sam."

"I'm not doing it to you, Suzie. I'm just not comfortable with this. I'm sure you can find another guy who would be happy to date Nora."

"It's just not the television thing, Sam. It's the match-making thing, too. My reputation is on the line! Please, help me out."

He guessed she was under as much stress about this as he. Squaring himself in front of her he said, "Suzie, it wouldn't be authentic. You don't want to come off as a fake. You want this to work. I swear I'm not the guy to pull this off."

Suzie stared right back and bit her lip. "It's the acting part, isn't it?"

"It's all of it. I'm not good at this sort of thing."

"But it will get easier."

"No."

"Oh, Sam." Her forehead curled into worry lines. "You can't. I…"

At that moment, Patricia stepped between them. "Sam, you're almost there. We just need a couple more shots. The crew thinks they can piece together an episode with what we have and a few carefully chosen shots."

"I'm not sure..."

Patricia put up a hand. Her New York attitude came out in a flash. "No excuses. You signed a contract."

Shit. That, he did. He studied Patricia's face, then Suzie's.

"Please?" she begged.

"Just a couple more scenes?" Why in hell he was caving, he did not know. Well, yes, he did. He was doing it for Suzie.

"Yes."

"Then I am free to go?"

"Of course."

"All right. Then I'm done." He headed back toward the picnic table, where a waiting Nora stood with a bottle of water.

On his way, he tossed a glance toward Becca, who immediately averted her gaze. Yep. She was watching him, too. A good sign and one that made him smile. But before he got three strides away, Suzie grasped his shirtsleeve and tugged. "Just get these scenes out of the way, Sam, and then later we can talk about the matchmaking part."

He didn't want to dwell on what she meant by that for too long. Him saying he was done was one thing. Suzie's interpretation of that, he feared, was quite another.

AN HOUR LATER, things still weren't working. Becca truly felt sorry for Sam because he was trying, but he couldn't act his way out of a plastic baggie. Nora, on the other hand, was acting her sweet little pea pickin' heart out. Of course, Nora could command attention in a soup can. But Becca wasn't sure how much of what Nora was doing was acting, or just her natural demeanor around men. It was her nature to lay it on a bit thick.

Patricia coached from the sidelines and Suzie just looked distressed.

Becca sidled up next to the author. "Not going so well, huh?"

"You can say that again."

Patricia leaned in. "We made a mistake doing this out in the wilderness. We need something to give it some pop. Nothing out here but mountains and trees and wildflowers."

"Sam is struggling," Suzie added.

"He's just not that into Nora."

"I could have told you that." Becca shrugged when both women stared her way. "Hey, I notice things."

"Too bad because she's into him, though," Patricia said.

"You think so?"

"Look."

Becca did. Nora was giggling and trying to feed Sam a piece of cheesecake. He sat stiff as a board, his mouth open, while she tried to pop a nugget in his mouth. She missed and laughed. Sam frowned and then catching himself, half-heartedly laughed, too.

For just a second he caught Becca's eye.

Nora then dipped a forefinger full of strawberry glaze and brought it her mouth. Her tongue snaked out and she slowly licked and then sucked. Becca's gaze went to Sam's face. His Adam's apple bobbed as he swallowed, then he turned his helpless stare toward the trio standing off to the side and said, "Suzie? Isn't this about enough?"

"Give him a break, Patricia. Certainly we have what we need now."

Thank God, Becca thought. She was almost embarrassed for Nora.

And Sam.

Patricia studied the scene before her, then glanced to her right at Suzie and Becca, and then back to Sam. "Sure. Okay. After just one more shot."

Everyone on the set groaned.

Everything around them went silent for a brief moment.

Abruptly, Patricia grabbed Becca by the arm and tugged.

"Makeup!" she shouted. "Suzie! Get that picnic basket and fill it up with food. Anything! Just put something in it. Nora! I need you over here, sweetie. Sam, Don't you move from that spot, do you hear me? I know we have one more shot in you."

Suzie scurried away.

Patricia dragged Becca toward the picnic table.

Nora stood with a deer-in-the-headlight look on her face.

Becca wasn't sure what the hell was going on.

And Sam looked like he could simply wither.

Then, before she realized it, Becca was overtaken by the make-up girl and being fluffed and buffed, while Nora was lead off by Patricia, whose lips were moving a mile a minute while Nora stood hands-on-hips, her head nodding, her eyebrows bobbing, and her nose wrinkling.

Becca looked to Sam. "I don't have a clue what's happening here."

"Just go with it," he said. "It's out of our control."

"Maybe we should just play and be nice, and then we can take our toys and go home soon."

"Promise?"

"One can hope."

"I'd like to go home with you and play with your toys."

Immediately, Becca flushed. And reddened. She was pretty darned sure. The makeup girl smirked and smiled, and buffed at her cheeks some more.

"Okay, so here is the deal." Patricia was back. "Sam, you stay where you are. Nora, take your seat again across from him. Suzie, give Becca that picnic basket. Becca, I want you to come sashaying in from the right and interrupt their lunch. I want you to flirt like hell with Sam, and Sam?" His head whipped her way. "I want you to flirt like hell back. We need some conflict in this matchmaking seduction scene, and this is the only way I know how to do it."

Conflict. Shit. Patricia Plum had no earthly idea how much conflict this was going to cause between her and best friend.

Nora looked at her with eyes round as buttered biscuits.

"Not my idea, Nora."

"All right!" Patricia clapped her hands, and the crew fell into their places. Suzie shoved the picnic basket into her hands and the next thing Becca knew was that some guy was snapping a clapper thing in front of her and shouting, "Action!"

In that instant, she knew there was only one thing left to do.

So, she did it.

She acted.

Plastering a huge grin on her face, she sashayed her ass over to the table, winked at Sam, and thought about one thing and one thing only—taking her toys home to play with Sam.

"I can't believe you, Becca!"

"What? It was acting!"

"Well, you didn't have to *act* so damned enamored with him. And you didn't have to *like* it so damned much!"

Rolling her eyes, Becca closed the cash register drawer. They'd been through this time and again. When would she stop? "I told you, Nora, it was all for the show. We'd been out there in the Indian summer heat for hours and everyone was tired. I just did what they told me to do so we could get out of there."

"Sitting on Sam's lap was totally uncalled for."

Oh, but it was so, so nice. Especially when he grazed his hand protectively over her back and massaged her neck a little. "Acting. Nora. Acting."

"I didn't know you had any interest in acting."

"I don't. It was Patricia. Wasn't my idea."

"You don't like him, do you? Please tell me you don't like him."

Becca sucked in a breath and faced her. *Shit.* "Of course not, Nora." She lied. Of course, she liked Sam. How could she not? But she couldn't tell her that.

Nora huffed out a breath. "All right. Then we're good." Bending to look under the counter she asked, "Are those cookies still here? I need to crunch something."

Crap. She'd tossed those a couple of days ago. "Um, I don't know..."

Nora rose and cracked her head on the counter. "Dammit!"

Oh, hell.

Becca went to her. "Nora, slow down. The cookies are gone. I'll go get you some if you need cookies. And please, don't hold it against me that Patricia tossed me into your television show. It wasn't my idea, remember?"

Rubbing her head, Nora frowned and pouted a little. "I know. He is really cute. I think I might like him."

Panic zinged straight through Becca. Deflect. *Deflect!* "Sam? Seriously? I didn't think he was your type."

Sighing, Nora replied, "Yeah, well. I think I do."

Damn. "But I'm not sure, Nora. You wanted me to give you my opinion and there it is. He just doesn't seem your type." *I'm not sure he's the one for you, Nora.* No. She couldn't say that because if she did, it would be for the wrong reason. Or would it be for the right reason?

"What do you think, Bec? That's the reason I had you come with me. What do you think about him? About Sam and me? Do you think I stand a chance?"

Oh, holy macaroni. What to say now?

"Well, he's older."

"I know, but perhaps more mature than the guys I usually date. I think I like him being older."

Becca smirked. Another tack. "Well, sure, if you like old guys. I bet he has a lot of relationship baggage though, being older and never married...."

Nora looked at her. Eyes wide. "You think?"

Shrugging, Becca returned, "Maybe."

Nora thought about that for a few seconds. "And maybe he's got all of the baggage behind him and he's ready to settle down."

"Or maybe he's too settled in his own ways and has no desire to be saddled with a woman?"

Nora knit her brows. "Saddled? You think that is what he would be with me?"

Closing her eyes, Becca shook her head. "No, Nora. That's not what I think. I just meant that maybe he is set in his single ways by now and likes it. He has to be in his late thirties. And you're at least ten years younger. That's a lot of distance. Practically a generational thing."

Becca watched Nora's shoulders relax. She stared off into the distance. Finally, she sighed and said, "I like older men. Always have."

Resigned, Becca turned away. "Sure. Right. I knew that." *Liar.* Whenever had Nora dated an older man? She fiddled with straightening some bookmarks on the counter.

"So you didn't really answer my question. What do you

think about Sam and me, Bec? Do you think I stand a chance?"

Swallowing hard, Becca turned back to her. "Nora, it just doesn't seem like he's..." She started to say, *like he's into you*, but then stopped herself. No use hurting her feelings. "Like the type of guy you usually go for. That's my only thought."

Nora bit her lip and stared across the store. "No, and perhaps that is a good thing. My type generally ends up breaking my heart." She fixed her gaze on something across the room, then broke away and looked straight at Becca. "But do you think he could *like* me? Be my Mr. Right?"

Becca searched Nora's eager face, and all she could do was pat her hand and say, "Sure, honey. I think there is always a chance."

Inside, Becca deflated like a kid's balloon on a hot sunny day at the park.

Chapter Five

Sam pulled another bag of mulch off the flat and loaded it into the back of the woman's small SUV. She smiled and thanked him and headed toward the driver's side of her car. Tugging at the handle on the flat, he backed away and turned toward the store. Sunday was always a busy day, especially in May, and today he was thankful for both the business and the physical energy it took to deal with customers.

Normally he would let one of the younger men do the loading, but today, he craved the mindless task and had taken over that job for a while. Loading customers' vehicles when they had larger purchases was a perk Haven's Hill offered over big box stores that sold plants and gardening supplies as a sideline. The other benefit was that he and his brother trained Haven's Hills employees to offer advice, ideas, and solutions. They even had computer programs that could sketch out landscaping plots and worked with customers to choose the right plans. All free of charge. They hired people who knew about plants and gardening and trained new staff personally. As a whole, they strived to be more knowledgeable than any other nursery around and shared that knowledge with their customers so they could make informed choices. Haven's Hill banked on the fact that customers simply couldn't get that type of support at a commercial store.

He and Jack desired to keep their clientele happy and convert them into returning customers. They strived to provide the human touch, respect the local flavor, and maintain their upstanding reputation—while working within a highly competitive regional market. Technology and social media were their friends, and their efforts seemed to pay off. Business this spring was already up twofold over last year.

Shoving the flat between the metal rails of the corral that held them just inside the door, he headed toward the back to see if anyone was getting ready to water. The afternoon was growing warmer. The plants would need a good spritz soon. Last thing he wanted was customers seeing gasping and dying plants on the showroom floor.

He rounded a corner and immediately came face-to-face with a woman pushing an overloaded flat.

"Oh!" The woman stopped abruptly.

"Trudy?"

"Oh, Sam! Lordy you practically scared the bejeebers out of me!"

He grasped her elbow. "I'm so sorry. Was sort of lost in thought there." He looked at her flat and gave it the once over —petunias and begonias, a Boston fern, two bags of topsoil, a large clay pot and saucer, gardening gloves, and a battery-powered weed eater. "Looks like you have your week cut out for you."

She grinned. "As always. You know I can't stop myself from digging in the dirt."

He grinned and then thought of Becca. She had said something similar about her mother, right? He looked at Trudy.

She eyed him back. "Everything okay, Sam? You look puzzled."

Nodding, he replied, "Of course. I'm fine." But he wasn't. Trudy North was Becca's mother. He'd known Trudy for a couple of years now—she was always in and out of the store—but until he saw her face-to-face this morning, he hadn't realized how much Becca looked like her. Immediately he was reminded of the pleasant afternoon he'd had yesterday once Becca had been thrust into the television show scenario.

He'd not been able to get her out of his mind since then.

"Well, you looked a little startled."

He grinned. "May I be honest?"

"Of course! You know me, Sam. I'm as down-to-earth as they come. I prefer your candid honesty over bullshit any day of the week."

He laughed. "Trudy, you are one of a kind."

"I strive to be. Now, what's on your mind?"

Pausing, he studied her. "I met Becca the other day. She was here about a week ago. I didn't realize you had a daughter."

This time it was Trudy's turn to study him. "My Becca? What on earth was she doing here?" Then she stopped, thinking. "Oh, pansies. Did she buy the pansies here?"

He nodded. "She did. Although at the time, I didn't think about your having bought pansies the other day, or I would never have recommended them. Hell, you about bought me out of them a few days earlier."

Trudy burst out laughing. "That girl was trying. She knows what I love. How she is mine, I will never know though. She is such a bookworm and hates getting dirty. Lord knows she did not get that from me. Probably from her dad. He did like to read, although he came in from the fields mighty dirty most of the time. He died when she was only five, you know."

Sam frowned. "No, I didn't know that, Trudy. I'm really sorry for your loss."

She stared off. "Me too." For a moment, she appeared to be in another place. Sam let her memories linger. Then she shook herself and looked to Sam. "But it's okay. Becca and I have had a good life and we are thankful. I love that girl like no tomorrow. Proud of her too. She just finished a double major in English and business. She's been away at college for the past few years."

So that's why he hadn't seen her around Harbor Falls. Before she left for college, she would have been just a kid and he wouldn't have paid any attention. Now, she was back and a full-blown woman—and yes, he was paying attention. What would Trudy think of that?

"I'm sure she's a wonderful young woman."

Trudy eyed him. "She is. If those degrees don't take her off to some big city somewhere soon, I'm hoping she'll meet settle down with a nice young man here in Harbor Falls one day. I sure would like to keep her and my future grandkids close."

Take her off to come big city someday.... "Is that her plan? To move away?" That notion bothered him.

Trudy shrugged. "I think it is a possibility. Lord knows I won't interfere in her life. I don't want her to go but I understand. The job at the bookstore is temporary, or so she says. She and Nora are close. Have been since they were kids. But she's been looking for jobs in Asheville and Charlotte. Or so she says."

No. "What do you think about that, Trudy? Do you want her to go? No bullshit."

"Honestly?" Trudy looked him straight in the eyes. "I'm hoping someone sweeps her off her feet before she finds that big job she thinks she wants."

∿

ON MONDAY, Becca pulled the gardening book off the shelf and ran her fingertips over the smooth cover. The author was one of those guys who had a television show on the Home & Garden Network. She didn't have a clue what his name was, although she knew that her mother most likely did. She paused to consider for a moment if this guy was really an average Joe, like Suzie from Harbor Falls, who happened to be at the right place at the right time and landed himself a TV show and a book deal.

She wondered.

As she stared at the handsome guy on the cover—who smiled back at her while knee-deep in pots and plants, crouched at the edge of a flowerbed, spade in one hand—her mind wandered to another gardening guy. Sam. Her heart pitter-pattered when she thought of him, even though she nearly always pushed the feeling away. She knew that Nora was hoping for another encounter with the landscaper and, well, she didn't want a thing to do with bursting Nora's bubble.

Even though she was having a difficult time getting those hazel eyes out of her head.

"If you are going to buy a book on gardening, I wouldn't recommend that one."

Startled, she yanked her head up to look at the person who had spoken.

"Sam?"

Oh yeah, Mr. Garden Man was standing square in front of her, all spit-shined and polished and looking rather gruff and outdoorsy—unlike the man on the cover of the book she was holding. She glanced over her shoulder, to where last time she checked, Nora was working in her office.

"What are you doing here?"

He took the book from her and began leafing through it.

"This guy has a great show," he began, ignoring her question, "but when it comes to putting things down on paper, he has a really odd way of doing it. Hard book for a newbie to follow, I think."

"Oh, well then, not the book for me."

The book snapped shut, and he handed it back. She shoved it onto the shelf.

"I was just browsing. I don't have a garden. The pansies were a fail." Why she felt the need to explain, she didn't know.

"Fail?"

"My, um, mother..."

"Ah. The one with the pansies. That's right. How did she like those?"

"Oh, fine." *Liar.*

"She didn't like the pansies?"

"She loved the pansies but she'd already planted a slew of them. She gave them to the neighbor."

"Hence, why you were looking at the book?"

"Yes. In a way. I need to learn more about plants..." *And I was thinking about you.*

Sam grinned again. Lord, she liked that.

"Good," he said. "Remember, I told you I'd teach you about plants. You just have to teach me about books. How about a recommendation?"

This was going in places she hadn't anticipated. "Book?"

"Yes. You know, to read?"

"Um, of course. Fiction or non-fiction?"

"Fiction, I think. I need to escape."

Escape what? Okay, she would play along. "The fiction section is over there. How about a thriller?"

"Will it make my spine tingle?"

You mean, like mine is right now? She stopped in mid-stride. "Sam?"

He smiled when she said his name. Dammit. "Yes?"

"Why are you here?"

He paused and perused her face for only a second or two.

"Well, it's a bookstore, Becca, and I just asked for a recommendation, so I guess I'm here for a book."

"I don't think so."

He arched a brow. "Then how about this? How about I take you to lunch?"

Her tummy nose-dived. "What?"

"I was in the neighborhood and thought why not? You have lunch plans?"

"Me?"

"Yes, you, silly."

"I... I don't think so."

"You don't have plans, or you don't want me to take you to lunch?"

Becca drew her lower lip into her mouth. "Um."

"Oh, come on, Becca. I promise I won't bite." He stepped closer, and the air between them seemed sucked away into a vacuum. Becca inhaled sharply. The sexy grin that went with his statement was almost her undoing. "We seemed to have a little energy flowing between us the other day at the shoot. Right? Let's explore that a little?"

Explore? And maybe I want you to bite? Shit! Stop thinking things like that, Becca!

Nora. Think about Nora. That's right. "Nora is around here somewhere, and I'm sure she's available."

He frowned and stepped back half a step. "Look, Becca. Please don't be mistaken here. I'm not here for Nora. That was acting. I'm asking *you* out to lunch, Becca."

"But..."

"What about the sandwich shop around the corner? That any good?"

Of course, it was her favorite place, but what *about* Nora? "That is not a good idea."

"Because?"

"Well, because of Nora..."

"There is going on between Nora and me, Becca. Nora isn't in this picture."

"I know, but Nora thinks there is a picture. And she thinks she is in it with you."

He stepped even closer. "Becca, I have made it very clear to Suzie that I do not want to be *matchmaked* with Nora."

She blew out a breath. Becca liked the sound of that. A lot. "Well, that's good." Yes, yes indeed it was. "But Nora still thinks...."

Sam's face suddenly tensed, with lines burrowing into his forehead. "She thinks what?"

Hell's bells, she was making him agitated. That was the last thing she wanted to do. "Oh crap. She likes you, Sam. And she still thinks that Suzie is going to try and fix you up again, and—"

Sam shook his head and grasped her hands. He glanced toward the office and lowered his voice. "Look, Becca. Let's get something straight. I'm not here for Nora. I'm here for you. I waited a while before I stopped by. When I saw you at Haven's Hill, I was immediately attracted to you. I know I came on a little strong, but hey, I don't flirt very often, and I was out of practice. Then, when I saw you again at the picnic, I couldn't very well ditch my supposed date and ask you out. So I waited. I have no obligation to Nora. Hell, I couldn't take my eyes off you! It took me a solid week to get up enough courage to come in here and ask you to lunch, so give me a shot here, okay? I'm doing the best I can."

Wow. Big speech. Impressive.

This was the place where she morally and ethically and calamari-vowly should be telling him to forget he ever saw her at the nursery, and during the picnic, because she was off men and had promised Nora. Even though Nora was breaking her calamari vow. And because she knew that her best friend still harbored a wee bit of hope that Suzie would find a way to hook them up again. This was the place where she should have said, *Sorry, Sam. I can't do lunch today*, and send him on his merry way.

But she didn't. Couldn't. For he was looking at her with big hazel-green hopeful eyes, practically willing her to accept his lunch offer, and dammit, she *wanted* to accept and forget the entire sordid mess because, wow, Sam Ackerman, was just too delicious and dreamy.

There. She admitted it. She liked the guy.

Hell. She couldn't like him because Nora liked him.

What to do? What to *do?*

Her stomach growled.

"See, you are hungry."

"Oh, not really, it's just…"

"Becca?"

"What?"

"If you don't agree to go to lunch with me, I might just have to kiss you silly right here in the thriller section."

So, kiss me silly, big guy. Just try it. "Oh?" She cocked an eyebrow at him.

He stepped closer, beaming. Becca tilted her face upward. Sam looked longingly into her eyes. "Let me kiss you," he whispered. "Just one, and then lunch."

"They have great fresh mozzarella, tomato, and sprout sandwiches around the corner. On rye."

He laughed. "Procrastinator. You're avoiding the inevitable, you know." A sexy come-hither grin broke across his face.

"I know," she breathed back. "Okay, let's do lunch."

He grinned, his mouth much too close to hers. "I'd much rather taste your lips," he murmured. And as he descended quite close to those lips a crackle of electricity passed between them, causing Becca's lips to twitch in anticipation. Then—

"Ack! Ack! *Ack!* "Screaming came from the office.

Sam jumped back.

Becca pushed off his chest.

Nora came running from the back of the store. "Becca. *Bec-ca!*" On three-inch heels, she slid on the hardwood floors, around the counter, and—

"Oh. My. *God!*"

"What the hell?"

Becca didn't like the look on Nora's face. She was white as a sheet. Racing past her, Nora went straight to Sam.

"Omigod!" she repeated. "Sam. Sam! Did you hear? Did you come in to talk about it? Did they call you, too? OMG! I can't believe it!"

"Believe what, Nora?" Becca took in Sam's face. He wasn't the least big excited. In fact, he looked, well, annoyed.

Nora turned to Becca and grasped her arm. "They want a second episode! With Sam. And guess what? They want another couple. So, of course I said the girl had to be you. They want you! Patricia said you were perfect. Now all we need to do is find another guy and we're set. We're going to be on TV. Again! Together!"

Then she shrieked again, hopped up and down, and grasped Sam by the shoulders, giving him a big squeeze. The look he gave Becca over Nora's head was one of frustration, confusion, and disbelief.

She was quite certain at that point that her emotions were rivaling the same. No way could she stomach lunch now. And she was pretty damned certain she would not get that kiss from Sam now, either.

"Yippee...?" She mouthed the word and twirled a finger in the air.

Sam caught her gaze over a bouncy Nora and rolled his eyes.

~

LATER, Sam sat at Suzie's kitchen table, stroking the fingers of his right hand through his hair. Repeatedly. "I'm telling you right now. Get me out of this."

She handed him a cup of coffee. He took it and cradled the mug in his hands.

"I don't know what I can do, Sam. Patricia is holding you to the contract."

"I signed for one episode."

"Well, yeah, but there is something about continuity."

Closing his eyes, he just wanted to make it all disappear.

"You don't understand, Suzie. This whole thing is interfering with..." My love life. Hell. Did it really matter? Perhaps he should just get the thing over with, and then he could pursue Becca to his heart's content.

For that is truly what he wanted to do. Pursue Becca and win her over.

It was more than that, somehow. He was drawn to her like he'd never been drawn to a woman before this. With Becca, he could see having the whole kit and caboodle. Make her his, get her pregnant with his children. Keep her in Harbor Falls so that Trudy could see her grandkids as much as she wanted.

"Nora is very interested in you, Sam."

Shit. He knew that but didn't know how to address it. He looked Suzie straight in the eyes. "You can't force what isn't there, Suzie."

"I understand that. I'm just asking you to be...flexible."

"Ah hell. I don't like the sound of that."

"I know. But Sam? My career as the matchmaking chef is on the line. I know you don't want to do this but..."

"Suzie," he interrupted, "I know you are supposed to be this matchmaking queen, but if I can be upfront and honest with you, Nora just isn't the girl for me. I'm not interested. Not in the least."

"So you don't want to try it another time?"

He huffed out a short, quick breath. "No."

Suzie sighed. "Well, I suppose people would see right through it, anyway. I'll have to come up with something else."

"I would very much appreciate that."

He took a sip of coffee and felt her gaze play over him.

After a moment, she said, "This is about Becca, isn't it?"

Now his curiosity was piqued. "You can tell?"

"I'm the matchmaking queen, right?" Reaching out, she laid a hand over his. "Leave it to me, Sam. I promise you. I will fix this."

He watched her eyes dart back and forth as she peered into his face. "All right," he said. "But fix it fast. I'm not a patient man."

Suzie tossed him a half-grin. "Got it. I won't drag out the misery."

"Thank God."

Chapter Six

"So I heard you ran into Sam Ackerman the other day."

Becca froze, her hands in the meatloaf mixture. It was Thursday evening, which meant it was meatloaf night at the North household. Meatloaf had been the Thursday dinner staple for as long as Becca could remember, and ever since she'd returned home from college, she and her mother had resurrected the ritual. She enjoyed spending the time with her. She loved her mother very much and felt lucky to have her. They'd lost her father way too soon.

But those words... The name of Sam Ackerman rolling off her tongue... Those words were the last words she expected to hear coming from her mother's mouth this evening.

"I, uh..." She picked up the ball of meatloaf mixture and transferred it to a baking pan. Vigorously pressing the meat into a loaf shape, she finally replied, "Um, well. Yes."

"Yes, you ran into Sam?"

She smacked the meatloaf with the palm of her right hand. "Yes. I met him. When I bought the pansies."

"Ah yes, the pansies. Cathy Baker is really enjoying them. I

hope you don't mind. I had no more room in the flower bed."
Trudy stepped up beside her, watching Becca work her hands
over the meat. "You can stop beating up the meatloaf now.
What's up with you?"

Becca stilled her hands and looked at her mother. "I like
him." Shew. She said the words.

After a moment, Trudy smiled. "He's a very nice man. I
like him too. Very helpful at the nursery."

Becca swallowed. "No. I mean yes. He was helpful. But no,
I mean I like him. A lot. You know. As a woman, I like him. As
a man. I'm not making sense, and it is problematic."

A slow grin spread across her mother's face. "In a strange
way, Becca, you are making perfect sense. And your liking him
is a problem?"

Biting her lip, Becca nodded. "Yes."

"Why?"

"Nora."

"Nora doesn't like him?"

"Oh no, Nora likes him just fine. As a woman"

"Ah."

"Umhmm."

"Well shit." Trudy leaned a hip into the counter and
crossed her arms over her chest. She studied Becca for a minute
then added, "But what does Sam think?"

Throwing up her meatloafy hands, Becca gasped, "He
likes me I think. Which is surprising you, know, because of
Nora. I mean, he asked *me* to lunch, not her. He almost kissed
me. He flirts with me. He is really nice, Mama, but Nora..."

Trudy took a breath, grasped Becca's arms, and squared
herself to face Becca. "But Nora nothing. Rebecca North, you
have been kowtowing to Nora Patterson since you were in
elementary school. You always thought she was prettier, more
popular, smarter—somehow you felt she was the one who
deserved the attention, not you. I don't know why but...?"

"Don't you get it?" Becca interrupted. "I didn't need the attention. Nora did. She thrives on it. I didn't *want* the attention. If people were looking at her, they left me alone. And it usually worked until—" She stopped.

"Until Sam?"

Becca felt like crying. "Until Sam. I don't know what to do, Mama. I don't want to hurt her but I like him a lot. And she's got him all tied up in this matchmaking TV show thing and well, I just..."

Trudy shook her head. "I know nothing about a matchmaking TV show thing but what I do know is this, Becca. Be true to your heart. Make yourself happy for once. Nora will survive."

"She's more fragile than me."

"And you've, in part, made her that way."

"Me?"

"Yes. Now look. She's stronger than you think. Give her credit and tell her the truth. And give yourself a chance. Hell, give Sam a chance. I think you two would make some kind of cute grandkids."

"Mama!" Becca was a little horrified at that statement. "You've just jumped miles ahead of me. There will be no grandchildren for you anytime soon!"

Trudy smiled and grasped the meatloaf pan, sliding it away from Becca. "We'll see about that. Now, go wash your hands and peel some potatoes. You know I like mashed potatoes and gravy with my meatloaf."

She sidled off and Becca watched her mother finish the meatloaf and put it in the oven. Children? With Sam? Turning toward the sink, she washed her hands with liquid dish soap and fantasized what life with Sam might actually be like.

Fact was, she would never know, unless she did the thing she didn't want to do.

But she had to.

She had to tell Nora.

SAM COULDN'T WAIT for Suzie to fix things.

He wasn't a very patient man and he'd been patient long enough. He was a man with things to do, places to go, and people—no, *a person*—to see. Becca. That's why he took matters into his own hands. He hoped to hell and back he was making the right move. After all, it was Saturday night. It had been five days, no six, since he'd seen Becca and he'd had no word whatsoever from Suzie that she had *fixed things*. He would not sit at home alone and mull this over any longer.

Becca could be out on the town. He could be interrupting a cozy date. She might be washing her hair. She might not want to see him.

But he was taking the risk anyway.

Lucky for him, Becca has signed up for his mailing list at the nursery when she was there a couple of weeks ago. Of course, he was probably not supposed to use that information for personal reasons but desperate times called for desperate measures.

He wasn't waiting any longer. He had her address.

Hell, what would she think? Him showing up here unannounced and uninvited?

The moment he lifted his fist to rap his knuckles on the wooden door to her apartment in the Old Harbor Falls neighborhood, his gut plunged and spiraled and he broke out in a fine sweat. He almost backed away and turned back toward the stairwell.

"You can do this, Ackerman. Full speed ahead." *I'm not waiting until next week when I have to see her in front of a whole slew of people.* He turned and headed back to the door.

He didn't want to wait any longer to spend time with Becca. He'd put off having a relationship for a while now. It was time to see move this forward.

Nora or no Nora.

SETTLED INTO HER COUCH, a cozy mystery in her hands, a cup of Earl Grey at her elbow, and a quilt wrapped around her, Becca idly turned another page. It was the perfect evening to end an ideal hermit-like Saturday afternoon and evening. She'd holed up and had been pretty much lazy, letting her head clear a little, while attempting to keep her thoughts from wandering into dangerous territory—territory that involved both Sam and Nora and about what she was going to do about the two of them.

About Nora. About Sam.

What to do?

She'd thought she had it figured out after she left her mother's last night. She would tell Nora and then tell Sam that she wanted to take him up on the interrupted lunch date offer. That she wanted to finish that almost kiss from the other day. But once she got to work this morning, and listened to Nora fret about the upcoming shoot, and how she couldn't wait to see Sam again, and how she just *knew* it was going to work out between the two of them, Becca changed her mind. How could she upset Nora's apple cart before this television shoot?

Becca would just have to wait a little longer to tell her—after all of this matchmaker stuff was said and done.

Now, though, she wished she'd gotten it over with. If she had, she might not be sitting here idly turning the pages of a book she really wasn't that into. Reading generally provided the safety net she needed. So far, that approach didn't seem to work this evening. She rarely read cozy mysteries but this new author by the name of Scott had seemed promising.

She had already read the last Calloway thriller and she didn't dare touch a romance tonight. No, not with her mood. This evening, she wanted to get lost in something entirely different. And something that didn't remind her one bit about her situation at hand.

I need to escape.

Yeah. Tell me about it.

It didn't seem to matter what she was reading, or thinking, or doing. Sam's words, or his face, or a mannerism clicked back into her psyche on cue. Didn't matter at all. He was just, everywhere.

Sighing, she turned another page. Had she even read the previous one? Oh yes, there was a murder, a woman pushed down the staircase, and the young heroine had rushed out of her bed and breakfast room to see her lying motionless at the foot of the stairs. Glancing about, she saw no one else. Slowly, she moved forward, descending a step at a time and picking up speed, keeping her eyes on the body to observe any sign of movement. As she reached the bottom of the stairs, the heroine bent to get a better look at the woman and....

A brisk knock rapped at Becca's door. She jumped and squealed a little.

Untangling herself from the quilt, she rose and glanced toward the clock. A little after eight. Nora, she knew, was having dinner with her folks. Her own mother was about ready to turn in for the evening. Early to bed, early to rise, was her mantra. It could be any number of other friends but they usually were busy on the weekends. Unless they were stopping by to drag her out of her cozy nest.

Well, she'd just quickly send them on their way.

The door unlatched and unbolted, she swung it wide,

expecting to see either Candy or Bea or Rachel, but instead she met eyes with....

"Sam?"

A hand went to her hair. Had she combed it lately? Glancing lower, she checked to see if she had on a stained shirt. Had she showered? Drat! Teach her to hole up and be a hermit.

"What are you doing here?"

"You look fine, Becca. May I come in?"

"Wha...?"

He brushed past her. Bold of him. She stood there with her mouth open looking like an idiot, likely.

"You might want to close both the door and your mouth, sweetheart."

With a swing of her arm and a jerk of her lower jaw, she did just that. Turning, she looked at him standing in the middle of her living room. "I'll be right back," she told him, taking in that wicked grin of his as she flew toward her bedroom.

Once there, she sucked in a breath and looked at herself in the mirror. Okay, yes, she had showered earlier. Good thing.

Her makeup was fading but heck, what did he expect showing up here like this? She usually didn't wear much makeup anyway.

The hair was fine. A bit tousled but that was okay. Her white T-shirt left a lot to be desired, so she stripped it off and found a bright red one, instead. Red was a good color for her. Her black workout pants would be just fine.

Looking at her feet, she was relieved to see that the pedicure she'd had three days ago was still in good shape. The red toenails matched her shirt. Nice.

Inhaling deep, she took another look in the mirror, held the breath to quell her flappable nerves, and then exhaled.

With steps much less hurried than the ones she came into the bedroom on, she walked into the living room.

Sam leaned back on the couch, reading her cozy mystery.

That sight gave her heart a little warm jump-start. He looked too damned good there. On her couch. In her apartment. In her life?

"Hi."

He put the book down. "Hi." Patting the couch beside him, he added, "Come sit next to me. Let's talk, okay?"

She nodded. "All right."

Likely, she sat way too close to him, for at the very instant that she did, his arm went around her and all she wanted to do was lean into him and put her head on his shoulder. He must have sensed that because he whispered, "It's okay. I'd like that."

She did, and he held her with both arms. Closing her eyes, she nuzzled into his shoulder and loved how it felt to be there. Wrapping his arms tighter around her, she heard and felt his exhale. She shifted closer. Together, it felt like they melted into one another.

It had been some time since a man had held her like this. The warmth that radiated from her chest toward him, and the all-encompassing feeling of him surrounding her, was something that she'd waited a long time for. Sam was worth waiting a long time for.

He moved a hand to her face and brushed her long hair back. She lifted her head to look into his eyes, while he made tiny, feathery strokes over her cheekbones and forehead. "I couldn't wait any longer to see you. I know I should have called but I was afraid you'd tell me not to come. You'd want to do the right thing, and in the process, you'd shortchange yourself. I know, Becca, that you are in an awkward position with Nora, but..."

"Sam?"

"Yes, sweetheart?"

"Please kiss me."

His gaze played over her face for only a second, and then he leaned in to touch his lips to hers.

Becca savored the firm, salty taste of his lips. He brushed them over hers, wet and hot and giving, and she knew at that moment if it were possible to get any closer to him, she wanted to do that. A very dangerous thought. With his fingers threaded through her hair at her temples, he held her still while he teased and played, and they mingled lips and tongues. A tingling sensation started at the friction and radiated through her. In her throat, her heart pounded.

Breaking away with a gasp, she whispered, "Wow. Some kiss."

"There's more, if you want."

"But you wanted to talk."

"I can talk with my lips."

"I'm not sure this counts as talking."

He shrugged. "Works for me." A bad-boy grin lit up his face.

Becca was lost. They should talk, yes, but this was magic. And she so needed some magic.

"Becca," he whispered while lowering her slowly to the couch, "let's relax and see what happens, okay? Let's lay here and talk and kiss and whatever else..." His voice drifted off as he nestled into the crook of her neck and laid soft nibbles there.

Whatever else was what worried her. At the moment, it appeared she didn't have a lot of willpower. But she had to resist him, didn't she? Even though she knew that, intellectually speaking, as his body crowded closer to hers, and she was cradled there between him and the back cushions, all she wanted was him.

All of him.

Maybe they should talk.

She fiddled with the placket of his shirt and sat up a little, pushing them both back up into a sitting position. "I am in a tough place, Sam. Nora is my best friend and my employer. Not that she would fire me, she wouldn't do that, but she likes you, and I don't want to ruin our friendship."

"Don't you think deep down she realizes that there is nothing between us? At some point, Becca, Nora is going to have to understand that. I mean, I've done nothing to lead her on. That television show fiasco should have made it apparent. We don't have a thing in common."

She agreed. "It's the fantasy of it all. That's just Nora. She's infatuated with the idea of being in love, and this matchmaking thing is so fairytale like. She's having a difficult time giving that up, I think. The thing is, Sam, she's been so wrapped up in her own world, she has no clue that there is a spark between us."

"It's more than that."

"What?"

"It's more than a spark. Don't you think so too?"

She did. But should she say that to him? "I do think there is something different, maybe special, more-than-spark-like happening between us."

He grinned and Becca's heart melted a little. Leaning in, he brushed his lips over hers. "Yes, definitely more-than-spark-like," he whispered.

Becca put her hands on his chest and pushed back a little. She wanted the kiss. More than anything. But they needed to talk. "I know, Sam. But it's more than that. It's the Suzie and Patricia thing, too, and the additional television show. They are all counting on you and Nora to make this work so Suzie has a good show, and Patricia is successful, as well, and..."

Sam placed a forefinger on her lips. "No, that's not what I

want to talk about, Becca. Between you and me. It's more than spark-like even, isn't it?"

More than a spark-like?

His fingers dropped to her collarbone. He dared to trace down to the center of her cleavage with a forefinger. A sexual thrill raced down her abdomen and lower. He whispered, "I can't get you out of my head. Haven't been able to for weeks. I want like hell to see if I can ramp up that spark. I want to fan it until it licks higher into some kind of erupting flame..."

Oh. My. God. Becca watched his eyes as he laid his palm flat on her chest and inched his fingers under the V-neck of her t-shirt.

His hand felt so, so good there.

This was moving fast. Way too fast. Wasn't it?

Was this what she wanted? To be with Sam this way? Sexually? Before they even really got to know one another?

Hell, she didn't want to make this another one-night stand, did she?

She whispered, "Will you still call me tomorrow?"

Pulling back, he looked into her face. "What?"

Her breathing deepened. "Whatever happens in the next few minutes, will I still hear from you tomorrow?"

Sam studied her. "I'm moving too fast. Look, Becca. I'm sorry. I should go. I shouldn't have come. I—"

Becca swallowed hard. "Answer the question, Sam."

His gaze narrowed. "If you are asking me if this is a one night, wham bam, thank you ma'am attempt for me to get into your panties, to love and leave you, and never see you again, then the answer is no, Becca. That's not my plan at all. And if that is the kind of man you think I am, then well—"

"Fan me," she whispered, the words barely falling from her lips.

Sam's eyes widened. "What?"

"Lick the flame, Sam. Ignite the spark."

"You're sure?"

She nodded. "I want you."

He stared into her eyes for a moment. "Ah, hell, Becca." He breathed the words. "I want you more than I've ever wanted a woman and once I have you, I don't think I'm ever gonna want to stop having you. You're sure?"

"Ignite the spark, Sam. I'm smoldering here."

Chapter Seven

Sam couldn't believe that at last, he had Becca in his arms and that she was like putty in his hands. He could feel her conflict, knew that it was there, but she'd given it over to something else. Him. He wouldn't take that for granted.

She angled her body and tilted her chin, offering her mouth to him. With her tongue, she reached out and sampled his lower lip, dragging the tip across it. Every nerve ending he possessed there cried out for more.

Hungrily, he took her mouth, deepening the kiss. They parried and thrust with eager tongues and heightened passion. She clutched him and kneaded her fingers along his back, bunching his shirt up in her fists. Groaning, he pushed her deeper into the couch, smoothing his hand down over her breast while he continued to claim her mouth. His palm cradled her breast inside the cup of her bra. Warm, full, firm...and ripe for his touch. The thought raced through him and settled in his gut. Damn, how he wanted her. Wanted it to be right, wanted to take it slow, wanted not to risk anything to make this go away. He needed Becca, and he didn't want to scare her off.

Lick the flame, she had said, and that surely meant that she wasn't scared, right?

He found her nipple and pinched with it between two fingertips. She moaned and thrust her tongue deeper into his mouth. He sucked and played, teasing her with his own. But he wanted more. A whole lot more.

He removed his hand from her bra and lifted the hem of her T-shirt over her breast. The cup of her bra rode low on her full breast, and he teased it away with his tongue. She had a perfect round areola, set dark against milky skin, tender and silky, ideal for sucking, licking...just right for him.

One flick of his tongue sent her arching into his mouth. He bore down, lifting her breast with a free hand and taking her fully.

Perfect, perfect. God, she was so damned perfect....

He needed more of her. Wanted her closer.

She must have been thinking the same thing for she was tearing at the buttons of his shirt. One by one, she unfastened them, stopping only long enough to allow him to strip her t-shirt over her head and unclasp her bra.

"Thank God," he hissed out. "Skin to skin."

"Yes."

Her breasts seared against his chest. "Damn, Becca. I never intended for us to go here tonight."

"Don't think, Sam."

"Probably we should think."

"No. Don't."

"But Becca, I don't want you to regret..."

"Flames, Sam. Lick them. Fan the flames."

If she said lick one more time, he was going to do just that.

"Now."

Before he realized it, he'd removed her pants, panties, too, and was smoothing his hands along her satiny smooth thighs and seeking the one place he knew that would be the source of so much pleasure for them both.

He knew it. But...

"Kiss me," she said. "Please."

When she said those kinds of things, he couldn't resist. He positioned her on the couch and perched himself straddle over her. He started at her mouth, kissing and sucking, then slowly and methodically dragged his lips over her body, giving equal attention to both breasts and those sinful nipples, first one and then the other. He laved tender affection and deliberate caresses over them until he had his fill. She whimpered and moaned, squirmed and arched... Lower, he traveled, to explore her cute belly button and then further, to the v-shaped curly patch at her center and the delicate, sensitive crease between her leg and hip. Sliding his tongue lower and then finally, settling between her thighs.

Her musk spurred him on, made him crazy with desire.

At the first touch of his tongue to the pearl between her legs, she jumped and called out. Her fingers grasped his hair, and she held him close. She was ripe and wet, and as his tongue played, he knew she would come fast.

And hard.

She shouted his name on the crest of her first shudder and panted repeatedly as he rode her until her tremors subsided and her legs fell back languid against the couch. He gave her a moment before continuing, lifting his face to watch hers. Her head lolled to one side, her hair fanned over one shoulder and breast, her face flushed, her breathing slowing.

He watched, and knew that he was falling hopelessly in love with this minx. From the first, she had captured his attention like no other woman. When she opened her eyes, reached out for him, and said, "Come here, make love to me," he knew he was over the top in love.

With as much haste as he could muster, Sam rid himself of

his clothes. He fumbled in his pocket for his wallet and removed the lone condom that had taken up residence there for way too long. He quickly took care of business and then ensuring no more time for a reality check, he plunged into her. Her legs wrapped around him, and her arms held him tight. He pumped into her, her silky insides drawing him deep. Nearly as ripe for an explosive orgasm as she, he knew it wouldn't be long before he would experience sweet release.

With his sweet Becca.

His. Becca.

The upsurge overtook him with unleashed abandon. He poured into her like it was his last dying deed and buried himself deeper inside like there would be no other chance to do so.

Shuddering, dizzy, and totally spent, he lay over her and savored the moment. Her hands gently caressed his back as his breathing evened. And all he wanted to do was possess her like this again, and again, and again....

It was Becca who spoke first, and the words she said weren't exactly the ones he had expected to hear. "I hope this wasn't a mistake," she murmured. Alarm coursed through him.

He loved her. This could never be a mistake, unless....

He didn't raise his head to look at her. "What do you mean?"

"It... So fast. Happened so fast."

"You wanted it, Becca, as much as I did." She shivered a little beneath him. "I would never have moved forward unless you hadn't encouraged me to do so."

"I know. I did. It's not that. I lost control. I just needed. Oh hell, what you must think of me."

She started to cry. Sam felt like a heel. And this was not how he wanted to feel at this moment. "Becca? I care for you. I think nothing other than that. What's wrong?"

"I... Oh hell, Sam. This was a mistake. Please, let me up."

No... No.

But he sat back and let her up. He wanted to argue with her. Wanted to tell her how much he loved her. Wanted to sweep her off her feet and take her home with him for the rest of their lives.

The look on her face, however, told him to back off.

"Becca, this will be okay."

"I'm not sure."

"You will be okay. Nora will understand." He stood and found his pants and pulled them on. She glanced about and found her yoga pants too.

"It's not about Nora," she said, slipping them back on. "It's about me. I shouldn't have let this happen. I shouldn't have been so eager. I don't want to break Nora's heart, of course, she's had enough heartbreak. But this..."

"This isn't about Nora, Becca. It's about us. You and me. We did nothing wrong."

She stared at him, not responding at first. "I... I'm confused. I like you. I don't want this to be casual. I don't do casual well. But I don't know if I want more, a relationship, and I... Oh hell, nevermind."

Casual? "Becca, this was far from casual." And then he added. "For me, at least."

Her face screwed into a puzzled mess and she glanced away. Couldn't make eye contact. What was going on here? Panic gripped him. "What are you afraid of, Becca?"

She rose and reached for her t-shirt, holding it in front of her. "I'm not afraid Sam. Of course, it is about Nora, in some ways. I don't have a clue what I will say to her."

"What about just saying, 'Nora, I'm seeing Sam. I hope you'll be happy for us.'"

"That's ridiculous."

"Why? I don't think it's ridiculous at all." By now, he was

convinced something else was going on. There was a little comfort in that. It wasn't about him. It was about something else. He continued. "Is that really what this is about, Becca? Or are you just afraid to try a relationship of your own?"

The stunned look on her face gave him his answer. "You should go now, Sam."

Bingo.

He dipped his head in a nod. "All right." He quickly dressed without saying anything else but before he left, he stepped closer and hooked his forefinger under her chin.

With only a slight tip of her chin, he angled her face toward his, but resisted the temptation to reach out and kiss her mouth. "Whatever you can't say, Becca, it's okay. I might walk out that door tonight but that doesn't mean I'm walking out of your life. This was not a one-night stand. Think about what's bugging you—and I'm pretty sure it isn't only Nora— and then let's talk. And truly, I mean talk."

He dropped his hand and her gaze lowered to the floor.

There was one more thing he wanted to say. "Oh, and Becca? Remember this. Whatever you think of yourself right now, forgot it. You're worth it. You deserve to be happy, whether you think you do or not. I don't regret one bit what happened here tonight and I don't think you should, either. In fact, I want to make love to you many more nights and not on your couch. Because I love you." Hell, the words fell from his mouth, openly and honestly. He did love her.

Finally, Becca lifted her face and looked into his eyes. Hers were misted over.

"Good night, sweetheart." Sam leaned in and kissed her on the forehead. "I'll give you space if that's what you need to realize that you love me too."

Then he, reluctantly, left.

❧

IT HADN'T BEEN the easiest week of her life. Sam was scarce. Her mother kept asking questions. And all Nora could talk about was the upcoming shoot at Suzie's. And Sam.

Sam. Sam. Sam.

Do you think Sam will like this dress?

I wonder what Sam will wear. Should I call him? Should we match?

Sam has the cutest butt, don't you think?

I wonder what our first kiss will be like?

Ugh. Becca wasn't sure how she'd endured five days of work with Nora without going crazy or blurting out, guiltily, that she and Sam had made mad passionate love on her sofa.

No. She couldn't. It would hurt Nora.

Now that the week was through, and she'd had time to digest the entire situation, maybe things were different now.

From her vantage point, standing in her apartment looking out her kitchen window looking over Old Harbor Falls, Becca figured there was only one thing to do now. Tell Nora. And she had to tell her before ten o'clock this morning, when they were due at Suzie's bed and breakfast, Sweet Hart Inn, to get ready for the shoot.

It would not be easy. To say the least, Becca was a mite tired of listening to every rehashing of the plans, but by later in the day, it would all be over.

Thank goodness.

Becca had a plan of her own. She was to pick Nora up in fifteen minutes to take her to the inn. Somewhere during that time, Becca planned to tell Nora the truth. Or, the almost-truth. She would leave out the details about what happened on her couch, but she would tell her that she and Sam were, sort of, seeing each other.

But was that a crock, too? Wasn't it?

She'd not seen Sam or talked to him all week. Of course, he

was giving her time, right? What had he said? Time to realize that she loved him too? Did she?

Of course, she did. She'd contemplated that all week too.

She loved him. How could she not? He had captured her heart from first glance at Haven's Hill a few weeks ago. Even though giving her space was difficult, it was a good thing. Her heart had grown around the idea of holding Sam inside it forever.

She loved him.

All the more reason to tell Nora the truth. The only way she would be able to move forward with Sam was to do it. Then she'd deal with her on insecurities.

Yes. Her mother was right. Sam was right. It was more than just Nora.

She'd let her one serious boyfriend rule her life.

She had let no one get close.

Since the wham-bam in the car with the match date, she'd been overcautious and unsure of herself. She hadn't ever wanted to feel like that again.

She'd gone from one extreme to another—letting a man control her life to reckless abandon with a man who only wanted to get off and move on.

But Sam wasn't like that. She knew that in her heart of hearts.

And she missed him. Her heart had ached all week. The only thing that kept her going were the last words he said before leaving Saturday night.

"No regrets" and "I'm not walking out of your life" were two things she'd held on to all week long. She'd searched her soul, pondering those statements. And of course, the three words, "I love you."

Becca moved out of the kitchen and into her bedroom. It was time for her to get moving. As she slipped into her jeans, her cell phone rang. Nora's name popped up on the screen.

"Hey, Nora. I'll be leaving soon to pick you up."

Nora jabbered from the other side.

"But I thought you needed a ride?" She listened for another few seconds. "Oh, okay. I understand."

She clicked off the phone and stared ahead. Nora was hitching a ride with Patricia, who had a rental car, so Nora could show her the way to Suzie's. Well, all right then. So much for GPS.

Confession time would just have to happen in some other way, but it had to happen today. She knew that in her heart of hearts. Maybe it was better for her to tell her after the shoot, anyway. Then all would go well with the show, Nora wouldn't be upset, and Patricia and Suzie would be pleased.

"And there I go again," she muttered to herself. "Working around things to make everyone else happy and not myself."

At least she realized why she was doing it now. That hadn't always been the case.

SAM PULLED into Suzie's driveway with a knot as big as his fist firmly embedded in his gut, right under his ribcage.

Sometime in the night, the thing had appeared, and by morning it was nothing more than a big, fat ball of bundled nerves. It had been nearly a week since he'd seen Becca but that didn't mean she wasn't constantly on his mind. She was. Both nervous about seeing her, and how they would get through this taping, as well as how she would react around him, was eating him up inside.

He arrived early, just so he could settle himself in for a few minutes before everyone else arrived. If he knew Suzie, she'd have some cinnamon coffee brewing and with any luck, that might quell his nervous stomach.

God, how he'd missed Becca. It was going to be hell not to run to her and fold her into his arms.

He used the back entrance, as was his usual custom, and found both Suzie and Brad milling around in the kitchen.

"Hey, man!" Brad greeted him with a handshake. He turned to Suzie. "Look at Mr. TV Man here, Suze."

Grinning, Suzie glanced his way while shuffling recipe cards and pouring a measuring cup of milk into a mixing bowl. "Yeah, he's quite our local celebrity, huh?"

"I'm afraid I'd rather leave that to you, Ms. Matthews."

"Not the TV type?"

"No, ma'am. I'm ready for this to be over."

"Oh!" Suzie glanced out her kitchen window. "Looks like the crew is here. There is a van and very nice car following them. Must be Patricia and Nora."

Sam groaned a little and followed her gaze. Yep, there they were. The van, the car and, yes, Becca's small sedan bringing up the rear. That ball in his gut clutched again.

"That's everyone," he said, to no one in particular.

"Nope." Suzie shook her head. "We have one more person coming."

Chapter Eight

Becca's fingers tatted nervously on her steering wheel. She had considered all the way out to the inn how she would handle things. Tell Nora now, or tell Nora later. Why did she keep wavering so? One minute she wanted to wait. The next she had a giant urge to tell her and get it over with, fearing if she waited she would lose her courage. She weighed the pros and cons of each, and every single time, she came up with the same conclusion—she didn't think there was going to be any good time to tell Nora.

Hanging back, she idled her car for a moment while the crew got out, stretched, chugged their last gulps of coffee, and began unloading equipment to carry into the house. She watched as Patricia and Nora talked quietly while they made their way up the steps to the back deck of the inn. Becca breathed deeply and exhaled. She'd already noticed Sam's truck, so he was here.

The butterflies that had overtaken her fingers earlier were now firmly ensconced in her tummy.

"Now or never," she whispered to herself and left her car.

Then louder, she shouted out, "Nora? Nora, wait up. I need to talk to you."

～

As the crew filtered in and out of the kitchen and dining room, setting up lighting and booms and whatnot, Sam worked his way to the fringes where he could watch both the back door and the happenings in each of the rooms. Patricia swept in and kissed Suzie on the check, shook Brad's hand, and smiled big.

"We've got a winner on our hands here, everyone. I know it." She nodded toward Brad and smiled. "I hope you are ready to pack your bags for New York because in another month, we'll be taping in the city."

Suzie's face beamed, and she jumped into her husband's arms. "I can't believe this! Little ol' Suzie from Harbor Falls. What a hoot!" She winked at Sam, and he was genuinely happy for her. Suzie had worked hard for many years. She deserved this crack at the big time.

"But right now, we've got other fish to fry," Patricia went on, fussing about the kitchen and lifting lids on pots. "Oh! What a beautiful marinara sauce. What are you going to do with that, hon?" She glanced Suzie's way.

"Vegetable lasagna. I figured something half-way hearty for the men and healthy at the same time."

"Good thinking." Patricia replaced the lid, and then swiped her hands on her black jeans. "So, Sam is here, and Nora and Becca are out back. Where is our fourth?"

"Coming," Suzie replied. "Coming."

A fourth. He'd forgotten about that. Sam swung his gaze back toward the kitchen door and onto the deck, where he caught sight of an animated Becca, flailing her arms about, and a noticeably upset Nora wiping tears from her eyes.

Shit.

~

"You what?"

"I never planned for it to happen, Nora."

"That's no excuse, Becca. Friends don't keep things from each other." She dabbed at an eye.

"I know. Calamari vows are not to be broken."

"Any kind of vow is not to be broken, but hell, that vow was not serious and you know it. And I broke it long before you. Damn, you went and worried all this time about me and Sam for nothing. Becca, I am so sorry. Truly, this is rather a hoot."

"It was serious to me!" At that moment, Becca realized she'd been hiding behind something that really was built on nothing more than vodka and seafood. She tossed her hands into the air. "But a hoot! My God! I've been worried for weeks about how to tell you I liked Sam. You kept talking about you and Sam, you and Sam..."

"Oh hell, that was a distraction. Trying to psych myself up for the acting role. I've been so nervous about this television thing. I really think I can do this, Bec. Can you imagine me being a reality television star? I didn't think you were taking me seriously, though. I knew all along Sam had an eye for you. Could tell that from day one, at the picnic."

"You brat, you!" Becca could barely believe her ears. Why had she been so damn worried?

"Did I tell you I had a date the other night with Max Carpenter?" A naughty smile crossed Nora's lips.

"No. Get out of town."

"Sorry, I meant to tell you."

"Vow breaker."

"I know."

"Did you have sex with him?"

"No!"

"Well then, I one-upped you."

Nora's eyes grew big, and she grasped Becca by the shoulders and shook her. Her voice rose. "You did what! You had sex with Sam?"

"Shh!" Becca put a hand over her mouth. "Not so loud!"

About that time, Sam opened the back door and stepped out onto the deck.

"Hey, girls! Whoa. What's going on here?"

Both women turned.

"Sam?"

"Take your hands off her, Nora. It's not her fault. No one needs to get hurt."

Nora's hands dropped to her side. "You don't understand, Sam. Becca was just telling me...."

"I know. I know." He stepped closer. Becca watched him look Nora straight in the eyes. He continued. "Nora, I'm really sorry, but I do not want a relationship with you. This matchmaking thing will not work. We can get through the show, but that's it. You just have to realize that. I'm in love with Becca."

Nora's mouth turned into an O, and her eyes grew equally round. Slowly, she turned her head to look at Becca. Sam shifted his gaze that way too.

"Well then," Nora said, "I guess you told me."

Sam glanced back at Nora. "I hope you understand."

"Sure." She giggled and looked at Becca, who felt giddy laughter bubbling up inside her.

"What's going on here?" Sam asked.

Someone behind them cleared her throat. Loud. "What's going on, Mr. Ackerman, is that you have just ruined my television show."

All bodies swung back to the open kitchen door, where Suzie, Brad, and Patricia all stood, framed in the doorway.

Suzie was wringing her hands.

Patricia wore a scowl on her face.

Brad gave him a thumbs-up.

"Ah, hell..."

Becca looked at Sam, who had uttered those words. Somehow, she was strangely thrilled that this was finally all out in the open.

"Wait." Suzie stepped forward. "There is something you are forgetting. This is a matchmaking show, and it is about couples, but that doesn't mean it's about Sam and Nora, and Becca and the other guy."

Patricia narrowed her gaze. "What are you talking about?"

Suzie smiled and glanced toward the driveway. "I'm talking about two equally sexy and viral men with hearty appetites. And I feel darned sure I can matchmake them both. Look."

A truck door slammed in the drive.

Up the walk stalked a man who looked a lot like Sam, but younger. Becca watched as he sauntered toward the back of the house with that same swagger. She glanced first at Sam, and then at Nora, who also was watching this young man with keen interest.

Oh, here we go again...

The man stepped up to the crowd.

Sam reached out his hand. "Jack. Welcome to the club."

The other man took his hand and shook it. "Can't leave all the fun to you, brother."

All the while, Becca watched Nora's face. She stared and bit her lip.

Suzie spoke. "Well then, we're all here now." She shifted her gaze to Nora. "Let me introduce you to Sam's brother,

Jack, Nora. I think you two may have a few things in common."

Nora tripped over her words. "Hi. Um, nice to meet you. Jack?"

He nodded and stepped up to Nora. "And you as well." He offered her his hand, and Nora gracefully took it.

They stepped off to the other side of the deck. Sam caught Becca's gaze and held it steady. *Is this over now?*

Chapter Nine

Much later that evening, after the taping was over, the crew had torn down the set, Patricia was on her way back to the airport, and Jack had offered to give Nora a ride home, Becca and Sam walked along the edge of Falls Lake bordering Suzie and Brad's property. As dusk fell, they held hands and glanced back up to the house further up the hill.

One by one, they watched the lights come on in the house.

Becca smiled at the simplicity of it all.

She wanted that. A life just like that. With a husband and children and maybe even pansies in the yard.

The days were growing warmer, but the nights were still cool. Sam put his arm around her.

"Let's sit on the dock and put our feet in the water," she said.

"Are you sure it's not too chilly for you?"

Becca shook her head. "Naw. I can handle it. Besides, we've been on our feet all day, and it might feel good."

They did. Becca leaned her head on Sam's shoulder while they savored the calm, watched the fish jump, and marveled at the Harvest moon hanging over the lake.

"Sam?" Becca whispered. "I want to talk."

Wrapping his arms around her, he pulled her close. "I know."

"You scared me," she breathed. "I couldn't believe the feelings I was having while we made love...and even before that."

"The last thing I want to do is scare you, sweetheart. I want you to love me and trust me."

Lifting her head from his shoulder, she studied his face.

"You said you loved me."

He nodded, smiling. "I've been around the block a few times, Becca, but I can tell you for certain, that until I met you, I'd never been in love before. I know this has been fast, but I love you with all of my heart."

Becca's chest got all tight and tingly, and her eyes stung a little.

"My last relationship didn't end so well," she told him, "and he was pretty much a control freak, so much so that I didn't realize until it was over how much of myself I lost. I've worked to build my life back and suddenly, I wanted to share it again, and it was just...scary."

He cupped her cheek in his palm. "We have all the time in the world, honey. Things have moved fast. Let's just slow down and enjoy falling helplessly and hopelessly in love. Sound like something you could live with?"

Becca peered deep into his beautiful hazel eyes. Nothing had ever felt so right in her entire life. "Sounds like something I could live with for a long, long time."

Sam smiled and kissed the tip of her nose.

"Oh, and Sam?"

"Yes?"

"I love you, too."

Want more Harbor Falls?

CONTINUE THE SERIES WITH THE HUSBAND
LIST.

Scroll on to read the first chapter!

The Husband List

MADDIE JAMES

The
Husband List

A *Sweet* Hart Inn Romance

Patricia Plum's Husband List

- Clean-cut.*
- Older than 35.*
- Has had at least one serious, committed relationship and must be ready to commit.*
- No kids.
- Absolutely cannot work in the Food or TV industry (and that definitely means *Channeling Food*).
- No ick factors (i.e. foot fetish, bad breath, sex in public places, etc...).
- Has to be drop-dead gorgeous. Clean-cut. Did I mention that?
- Has an established, lucrative career/business/profession—in other words, supports self/has money.*
- Catholic.*
- Must love sushi.*

*non-negotiable

Chapter One — The Husband List

Suzie Matthews breathed deep, held that breath for two full seconds, and then relaxed with a lengthy sigh. Staring at the Manhattan high-rise to her right, her gaze steadily rose as she peered out from the grimy cab window. The light changed and the cab jerked, her body scooting forward with it, then falling back against the seat.

Music and words circled inside her head.

Start spreading the news...

Da-da-da-dA-Daaaa.

I want to, da-da-DA-da-DA, New York, New York...

"I'm a part of it," she whispered.

"What honey?"

Suzie hadn't realized she'd said that out loud. Glancing to her left, she took in Patricia Plum's smile. Patricia was her newly-appointed producer of her debut television show, and was quickly becoming a very good friend.

"Nothing. Just mumbling to myself."

"Ah." Patricia turned to look out her window. Suzie followed suit on her side of the cab. "Can you believe you are here?"

Inhaling deep, Suzie smiled at the window. "No. No, I can't."

It had been a whirlwind, fairytale time. Three years earlier, she was struggling through a divorce and trying to start her cooking classes and Sweet Hart Inn, all while writing her first cookbook. Then Brad came back into her life and they had their little boy, Petey, her cookbook became a bestseller, and now...now *this!* Her own television show!

"Pinch me."

"Believe it, sweetie. Life is good."

She glanced again at Patricia, whose head rested against the back of the seat. Her eyes closed, she wore a slight smile on her face.

"Good for you, too, Patricia?"

She nodded and smiled bigger. "Your *Matchmaking Chef* show is going to be hot. It's going to be good for all of us. I am so glad I discovered you!"

Then, Patricia started humming from her side of the cab.

Suzie guessed happiness was catching. Patricia did seem quite cheerful yesterday when she had picked Suzie up at the airport and as they shared dinner last night. She was excited about the show, of course, but there was a simple calm about her—not the frenzy they had all experienced back home in Harbor Falls during the first shoot. She was totally different. Relaxed, maybe.

Perhaps it was because Patricia was in New York. In her element.

She smiled at her new friend's off-tune humming. It was a different song from Suzie's, although she couldn't quite make out what it was, because her own tune kept running through her ears.

Earwigs, they call those. Right? When you can't get a song out of your head?

Ba-da-dA-da-Daaaaaa...
Start spreading the news...

"I'm gonna be a star," she whispered, absolutely certain she was up for it.

The pointed toes of Patricia Plum's candy apple-red Jimmy Choo heels tapped out a rhythm on the vinyl floor mat. The darned tune got stuck in her brain two days ago when she'd come up with a harebrained scheme that she had yet to slide by Suzie.

Ta-ta-ta, Ta-ta-ta, Ta-Ta-TA-TA!
Ta-Ta-TA-TA! Ta-Ta-TA-TA!

The cab rounded a corner, a little too sharp, and she opened her eyes to glance out at the street. Simultaneously, she rapped on the Plexiglas between them and the driver.

"Hey! I said straight to 5th Avenue. Don't go this way!"

"Slight detour, miss," he rattled out. "Traffic."

"No. No." She glanced at Suzie who had now turned and was watching her. "Pull over. Let us out here. We can walk."

The cabby shrugged and did as she asked. Patricia glanced at the meter, tossed him a scowl and enough cash to pay for the ride plus a small tip. She pushed Suzie out the passenger side door.

Scrambling, they reached the sidewalk and both women exhaled.

Patricia watched Suzie, who was looking up—always was looking up, it seemed, since she'd arrived in the city the day before. She linked her forearm at the woman's elbow. "It's a beautiful day to walk and it's not that far now."

Grinning, Suzie nodded her agreement, which warmed Patricia's heart.

"Besides," she added, "you're in New York. We walk everywhere here."

She didn't know why she was taken so with this country cook named Suzie Hart Matthews, but she knew beyond any shadow of a doubt that she and Suzie would be fast and long friends. She also knew that Suzie was bound to be a star.

Ever since their weeks in Harbor Falls, they'd clicked like peas.

And the pilot they'd shot for her show went over famously.

Patricia was going to have a kick showing her new protégé the finer points of New York City. Particularly, the cuisine.

Not to mention, the men.

Not that Suzie needed a man. She had the hunky, sinful Chef Brad wrapped around her delicate fingers. But Patricia was lacking in that department, and if Suzie's matchmaking skills were as good as they say, and as she suspected... Well, time would tell.

She'd think more about that later.

They walked arm-in-arm. Suzie still grinned in awe. Was she humming, too? Patricia strained to hear. Ah, yes, she was.

Happy.

Everyone was just happy!

Her own tune invaded her head again, and she sang to herself. Why not?

Matchbaker, matchbaker, bake me a match...

No. *Make* me a match, she thought with an inward giggle. But bake me a match was much more appropriate.

Shit! What a great jingle for the show.

Brilliant. She was just, brilliant.

This was going to go well. All worries aside. Now, on to the studio.

The duo marched forward. Glancing to her right, she

asked, "Are you ready for your first day at work, Ms. Suzie the Matchmaking Chef?"

"I'm scared as hell," Suzie shot back. "But ready to dig in."

Patricia knew exactly how she felt.

Learn more about *The Husband List* on my website, or purchase at your favorite bookstore.

A Note From Maddie

Friends,

I hope you enjoyed reading *Miss Matched Hearts*. I love that Becca got her man, and Sam is such a hunk! But will Nora finally get her man? (Check out the Falls Mountain books to find out!)

If you enjoyed this read, then please consider sharing with others. One of the best ways to tell others about the book is to leave a review at Goodreads, or at the bookstore where you purchased the book. You can also leave reviews at my website, maddiejamesbooks.com.

Ready for more Sweet Hart Inn? Scroll on to read the first chapter of *The Husband List.*

Will Suzie find the right man for her publicist, Patricia Plum?

More Sweet Hart Inn

Cozy up at the inn where the heart of the Blue Ridge beats strongest...

Welcome to Sweet Hart Inn, a charming bed and breakfast nestled along the peaceful shores of Falls Lake, at the foot of Falls Mountain. At the center of it all is chef and innkeeper Suzie Hart, whose kitchen is always warm, and whose heart is always open. Together with her husband Brad, Suzie serves up matchmaking advice and comfort food, along with second chances, and a generous helping of happily ever after.

The Sweet Hart Inn Books

All of My Heart
Take My Heart
Match My Heart
Tame My Heart
The Dating Game
Miss Matched Hearts
The Husband List
Chase My Heart
No Sweeter Match
One More Kiss

The Falls Mountain Books

Welcome to Falls Mountain, and the quaint town of Harbor Falls.

Tucked deep into the Blue Ridge Mountains, bricked streets, lakeside views, and charming local shops set the scene for small town romance.

In this standalone-but-interconnected series, you'll meet bakers, bookstore owners, chocolatiers, school teachers, and more—all trying to run their businesses, chase their dreams, and keep their hearts in check. But in Harbor Falls, love has a habit of showing up unannounced...

From second chances to secret babies to grumpy-sunshine pairings, each book brings a satisfying happily-ever-after and a cast of characters you'll want to visit again and again.

Falls Mountain Romance is a companion series to the Sweet Hart Inn Romance books by Maddie James.

Dance into My Heart
The Christmas Nanny
The Heartbreaker

Star Crossed
Not This Christmas
Convince My Heart

I hope you'll check out these books, and my other series, on
my website at:
www.maddiejamesbooks.com

About Maddie James

Romance with a pulse—small towns, big love, and a dash of drama.

Maddie James writes small-town romance with heart, heat, and the occasional haunting. Her stories range from sweet to spicy, suspenseful to supernatural—happily-ever-afters guaranteed! From stand-alone love stories to binge-worthy series, Maddie delivers love next door, some cowboy kisses, an occasional hint of danger, and just enough drama to keep things interesting.

Get all the drama delivered to your inbox when you sign-on to Maddie's VIP reader list!
Free books, sneak peaks, bonus content, giveaways, and more...
Learn more: maddiejamesbooks.com/pages/newsletter